CHILDREN'S CLASSICS
EVERYMAN'S LIBRARY

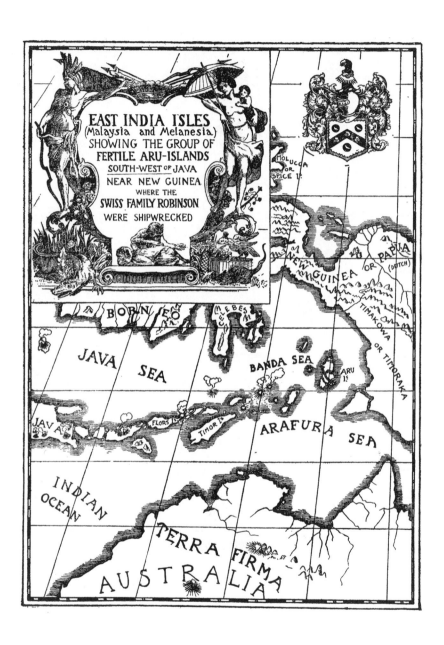

EAST INDIA ISLES
(Malaysia and Melanesia)
SHOWING THE GROUP OF
FERTILE ARU-ISLANDS
SOUTH-WEST OF JAVA
NEAR NEW GUINEA
WHERE THE
SWISS FAMILY ROBINSON
WERE SHIPWRECKED

Johann David Wyss

The Swiss Family Robinson

With Illustrations
by Louis Rhead

EVERYMAN'S LIBRARY
CHILDREN'S CLASSICS
Alfred A. Knopf New York Toronto

THIS IS A BORZOI BOOK
PUBLISHED BY ALFRED A. KNOPF

First published 1812
First included in Everyman's Library 1910

Design and typography © 1994 by David Campbell Publishers Ltd.
Book design by Barbara de Wilde, Carol Devine Carson
and Peter B. Willberg

Seventh printing

Five of Ernest H. Shepard's illustrations from *Dream Days* by
Kenneth Grahame are reprinted on the endpapers by permission
of The Bodley Head, London. The sixth illustration is by
S. C. Hulme Beaman.

All rights reserved under International and Pan-American Copyright
Conventions. Published in the United States by Alfred A. Knopf,
a division of Random House, Inc., New York, and simultaneously
in Canada by Random House of Canada Limited, Toronto.
Distributed by Random House, Inc., New York

www.randomhouse.com/everymans

ISBN 0-679-43640-5

Typeset in the UK by AccComputing, North Barrow, Somerset
Printed and bound in Germany
by GGP Media, Pössneck

CONTENTS

CHAPTER I

SHIPWRECKED!

F OR SIX days the storm had raged wildly, and our situation became more dangerous every hour. Driven out of
our course, we no longer knew our position, and the ship had
lost her masts and was leaking.

Down in our cabin my four sons clung fearfully to their
mother, and to all of us it seemed that the end was near.
Then, suddenly, came a cry from above – 'Land! Land!' But
almost at the same moment we felt a sudden shock that
seemed to shake the vessel asunder, followed by a fearful
crash. With sinking heart I realized that we had struck a
rock.

'Lower the boats!' I heard the captain shout.

Hurrying on deck I was startled to see that the ship's boats
were already dangerously overcrowded, and that it would be
almost impossible for us to find places. Buffeted by the wind
and half-blinded by the spray, I crossed to the side of the
vessel, but I was only in time to see the last rope cut, and the
next moment a mighty wave had separated the boats from
us, and had driven them far beyond our reach. In my despair
I shouted wildly for help, imploring them to return, but my
voice was lost amid the roar of the storm, and soon nothing

was to be seen of the retreating boats but two dark specks that now and again appeared on the white surface of the ocean.

All chance of escape now seemed gone for ever, and I was about to resign myself to certain death, when, turning my eyes southward, I was overjoyed to perceive a coastline stretching along the horizon. Thither, from that time, all my hopes were directed.

My family, who had heard my cries for help, rushed on deck, and their anguish, when they realized our situation, was greater than my own had been. Forgetting our real helplessness in my new-born hope of reaching the island which I had just discovered, I tried to reassure them.

'Take courage!' I said. 'Our cabin is so fixed as to be beyond the reach of the waves, and land is not far off. If the storm should abate during the night, it is possible that we might reach it.'

My children, with the confidence of their age, now cast their fears aside, and looked forward joyfully to certain deliverance on the morrow. As the evening advanced the storm increased in violence. My three youngest children, who were quite exhausted by the anxieties of the day, fell fast asleep; but Ernest, my eldest boy, who was able fully to comprehend the dangers of our position, remained up with me to help me in my search after bladders, casks, or anything that would serve as buoys, by means of which we might reach the land should the vessel break up during the night.

Having found several empty kegs, and having joined them firmly together in couples, we fastened them under our arms, and thus we hoped, in case of emergency, to float ashore. These precautions taken, Ernest too was overcome by fatigue, and my wife and I were left alone to pass the night in prayer.

As morning dawned the storm began to abate; the sea became calmer; the wind fell, and a glorious sun shed his golden rays over the troubled surface of the waters. Delighted by the change, I summoned the boys on deck.

Ernest, who was always ready for instant action, proposed that we should explore the ship, as we were sure to find many things on board which would be of use to us should we ever reach land. Acting on his suggestion, I sent them all on a voyage of discovery to the hold of the vessel, and as they started eagerly on their mission each vowed to bring back just the thing that was most required.

A few minutes after I heard a cry of 'Papa, they'll bite me; I'm afraid!' and saw little Jack appearing on deck holding on bravely to the collars of two huge dogs, which were making frantic efforts to jump on him and lick his face. This was their manner of testifying their gratitude to their deliverer, who had found the poor half-famished brutes shut up in the captain's cabin.

'Well, Jack,' I said, as I relieved him of his charge; 'I don't think your discovery will benefit us much at any rate.'

'I know that, papa,' he answered, ruefully; 'but the poor animals looked so hungry, I could not find it in my heart to leave them below; besides, they will be very useful to us for hunting when we get on land.'

'You are right,' I said, 'but have you thought of how we are to get there?'

'Oh yes!' he replied. 'I have heard of people making rafts at sea, and have been thinking that we might do the same if we could find some boards and ropes.'

'A very good idea, Jack, and one we must try to carry out; but here come the others! Let us see how their search has been rewarded.'

When the boys displayed their treasures, I was quite astonished to see the number of useful things which they had collected, and how wisely their selection had been made with a view to our future wants. Amongst other things I noticed, with joy, fowling-pieces, fish-hooks, powder and balls – for I knew that on these we should be dependent for our food; nails, hammers, saws, gimlets, and other carpenters' tools had likewise not been forgotten. As for my wife, she announced triumphantly that she had found a cow, some sheep, and several goats just in time to save their lives, for, as they had been neglected during the storm, they were almost famished.

We now began to think of constructing a raft, by means of which we might reach the island, which, since the clouds had partially cleared away, could be distinctly seen against the horizon; and we all started for the hold again in search of anything which we could make do service as a boat.

The only things to be found, which were at all suitable for our purpose, were four wooden casks firmly bound with iron. These we sawed in halves, and having placed the eight tubs side by side and joined them tightly together, we nailed them to a strong plank. Two other planks were then fastened along the sides of the tubs and brought to a point at each end, so that the raft might cut the water easily; while, to prevent its being overturned, a balancing pole, to which some empty brandy casks were tied, was fixed at each end of the strange vessel, and the work was completed.

With some difficulty, and not without help from a power-ful lever I found on board, we launched our bark. The children, who felt very proud of their handiwork, were anxious to embark immediately, but, as the evening was advanced, I decided to remain on the wreck another night, and try to reach land on the following day, should it be sufficiently calm.

The sun shone brightly the next morning, and everything seemed to favour our removal, so, gathering together whatever we thought might be useful to us in the future, we were about to trust our lives to the raft, when the crowing of the cocks, which we were leaving behind, attracted our attention. At their mother's request the children returned for the hens and pigeons, which they placed in a large wicker cage, while the ducks and geese were set at liberty in the hope that instinct would guide them to land. Having carefully provided the animals on board with food and drink enough to last them several days, and having loaded the boat with ammunition, food, carpenters' tools, canvas for making our tent, and as many other useful things as I could make room for, we embarked. My wife occupied the first tub; in the second sat Jack, a boy of eight years of age; in the third the six-year-old Franz; the powder, sailcloth, and fowls were stowed away in the fourth; the victuals in the fifth; the sixth held Fritz, now fourteen years old; the seventh, Ernest, who had just attained his sixteenth year; while I occupied the eighth, and endeavoured by means of a pole to steer our wonderful vessel.

As the dogs, Topsy and Bill, which had been left on the wreck, saw the raft slowly retreating, they sprang whining

into the water and soon overtook us. But as, on account of their size, it would have been dangerous to take them on board, they swam after us, now and again resting themselves by placing their forepaws on the casks that were fastened to the balancing poles. Thus we reached the island.

From a distance it presented a very barren appearance, and nothing could be seen but a line of rocks extending the whole length of the coast. On a nearer approach, however, trees, which we guessed to be palms, were visible not far from the water's edge; and by the aid of a small telescope, which Jack produced from his pocket with no small amount of pride, I could see that the land was not nearly so sterile and uninviting as we had at first feared. A little creek which served as a landing-place was soon discovered, and at last we set foot on the welcome soil.

Our next anxiety was to find a suitable place to erect a tent where we might pass the night in safety. Ere long this also was found, and soon, by means of poles, which we fastened in the fissures of the rocks, and sailcloth, with which we had provided ourselves before leaving the wreck, our temporary habitation was constructed. Some moss and withered grass, which the boys had gathered and spread out in the sun to dry, furnished us with pillows, and our arrangements for passing the night were complete.

While the boys were occupying themselves inside the tent, I collected a pile of stones on the margin of a stream which ran near us, and built a sort of fireplace, in which a huge fire

of dried sticks and twigs was soon crackling pleasantly. My wife, with a view to appeasing our hunger, placed on the rude grate a pot of water, into which I threw a few pieces of the portable soup that we had found among the cook's possessions; and soon the savoury odour of the preparation told us we might expect a palatable dinner, for which we were beginning to feel the necessity.

Meanwhile Fritz, who had been well accustomed to the use of firearms among our native mountains in Switzerland, loaded his gun and proceeded along the banks of the stream which flowed close by, in search of something with which to stock our larder; Ernest also set out, but preferred to take the opposite direction; while Jack, who was less ambitious than the others, contented himself with climbing the rocks in search of mussels, for which he had a strong partiality.

They had not been long gone when I heard a cry of terror, and, seizing my axe, I rushed in the direction from which the sound proceeded, prepared to find that Jack had got into some new mischief. The sight that met my eyes, however, was more laughable than terrifying, but my appearance was evidently a relief to the boy, who called out when he saw me approaching, 'Papa, papa! please come fast; I have caught a terrible animal.' Looking into the water, in which he stood up to his knees, it struck me that the 'terrible animal' had caught him rather than he it, for a huge lobster held him tightly by the leg, and all his efforts to free himself from its clutches were fruitless.

A slight blow from my hatchet soon made it release its hold, however, and catching it by the back I brought it on shore, much to the delight of the other boys, whom their brother's cry of terror had summoned to the rescue.

Now that all danger of another attack from the enemy seemed over, Jack, burning with anxiety to be himself the bearer of the prisoner to his mother, caught it eagerly with both hands; but scarcely had he touched it, when he was warned not to play with edged tools by receiving a sharp blow on the face from its tail. A renewed howl of anger and

fright burst from him as he threw the lobster violently on the ground, and vowed never again to touch the 'ugly brute.' Taking the animal again by the middle of the body, I showed him how his own carelessness had brought its punishment, and that by holding it properly it could be rendered quite harmless.

Having shown my wife what Jack proudly called his 'captive,' Ernest suggested that it should be utilized at once and thrown into the pot, as it would much improve the flavour of the soup which was in course of preparation. Our housekeeper, however, did not look favourably on the recipe, and preferred to reserve the animal for future use. She suggested to Ernest, though, that if he desired to render our meal more enjoyable, he should procure a little salt, as that was the only ingredient the soup now required in order to make it palatable. He ran off quickly in search of this valuable commodity, which he assured us he could easily find, as he had seen it lying in handfuls in the fissures of the rocks where the sun had dried the sea water.

He proved his assertion, too, by bringing back a good quantity of the desired article, but it was so mixed with sand and seaweed that I immediately pronounced it useless. My wife, however, dissolved it in fresh water, and, having filtered it through a piece of canvas, managed to improve the flavour of our dinner wonderfully thereby.

Our meal was at last ready, and we gathered eagerly round the pot, anxious to satisfy our appetites, which the morning's work had rendered ravenous. But a new difficulty here presented itself. The soup was there to be eaten, and we were anxious to eat it, but without plates and spoons, or anything to supply their places, how were we to manage?

'If we had some cocoa-nuts,' suggested Ernest, 'we could make spoons from their shells.'

'Quite true,' I answered, gravely; 'and if we had a china dinner set and a dozen of soup ladles we might tide over our difficulty beautifully, but the one is as much beyond our reach as the other.'

'How would mussel shells serve our purpose?' asked my wife. 'I saw Jack playing with some a little while ago; perhaps they might do.'

'Capitally,' I replied, 'if we can only get some. Jack might lead the way to where they are to be found.'

The children ran off and soon returned bringing a good supply, and this difficulty overcome, we sat down thankfully to our first meal in our new home.

Soon the sun sank behind the horizon, and the darkness

which immediately succeeded showed me that we must be near the equator. The increasing chilliness of the air warned us to betake ourselves to the tent, whose protection from the cutting night-wind, which had suddenly sprung up, was exceedingly welcome. The storm had now completely abated, and the sea, as if exhausted by its own fury, lay calm as a lake. Everything seemed to invite repose.

Morning had scarcely dawned when we were awakened by the loud crowing of the cocks that were perched over our heads, and I began to consider how we should best occupy ourselves during the day. Our first duty seemed to be to ascertain, if possible, the fate of our shipmates, who had abandoned us to almost certain death when they set out from the wrecked vessel, and also to explore the island and fix upon the best place for our future habitation. It was finally decided that Fritz and I, accompanied by Topsy, should start on this voyage of discovery, while my wife remained in the neighbourhood of the tent with the other boys. They wanted to come, too, and long after we had disappeared from their sight we could hear their shouts of farewell and encour-agement, which were only drowned by the murmur of the river which we had now arrived at.

The banks of this river on either side were so steep and inaccessible that we were obliged to proceed for a long distance towards its source before we could find any place where it was possible for us to cross. At last, however, we reached a narrow bend near a pretty waterfall, and here, by using pieces of broken rocks as stepping-stones, we were enabled to gain the other side in safety, and soon had reached the shore of the bay. Here we brought Jack's telescope into service, and scanned the horizon eagerly, hoping to find some trace of the boats which had borne our companions from us. But not a speck was to be seen on the restless waves, and our fears that they had not survived the storm now became certainty.

Descending from the rock on which I had climbed, I was astonished to see Fritz lying at full length on the sand and examining something with apparent anxiety. My amazement increased when he suddenly cried out, 'The island must be inhabited, father; here is the print of a man's foot in the sand.' Gazing at the place where he pointed, I could distinguish what looked like the mark of a naked foot partly obliterated, but as only one could be discovered, I did not feel alarmed, or inclined to adopt Fritz's fear of savages.

'You know, father,' he said, 'if there were such on the island they would look on us as intruders, and I don't think our lives would be worth much in their hands.'

'The possibility of natives being near us must make us more careful about where we go and how we are armed,' I answered. 'With a good gun for my companion, I should have little fear of coming off best in an encounter with one of them.'

Pursuing our course silently, we directed our steps inland, and arrived after a two hours' march at a small plantation, where we sat down on the grassy bank of a little stream that flowed softly among the trees. After a rest we went on again, and suddenly Fritz stumbled over a large round substance which turned out on examination to be a fine cocoa-nut. I welcomed it gladly, as I expected it to provide us with refreshing drink. Unfortunately, though, on opening it, we found nothing but a withered kernel unfit to be eaten.

'How is this, father?' asked Fritz, in a tone of disappointment. 'I have heard a great deal of cocoa-nut milk which travellers prize so highly, yet there is no such thing in this one.'

'It is only when the fruit is plucked half-ripe from the tree that it is found to contain the much-lauded beverage,' I replied. 'When allowed to ripen, the liquid becomes hard, and if left to fall off the tree it decays, as you see this one has done.'

Fritz continued his questions as we resumed our journey, but while seeking information he was also on the look-out for some new discovery. His watchfulness was at last rewarded by the sight of another vegetable wonder which he called me to examine. I was greatly pleased to see that it was a fine specimen of the gourd tree, and that many of the same species were growing close at hand.

'This tree, which bears its fruit in the trunk, is likely to be of great service to us,' I said. 'Out of the shell all sorts of vessels can be formed. We can even use it for making cooking utensils, as I am told the savages are accustomed to do.'

'But the shell is quite frail, apparently, father; and how could it bear the heat of a fire under it?'

'It is not placed on the fire, my son,' I answered, 'but is filled with water, and red-hot pebbles are thrown in one by one. In time these cause the liquid to boil, and the pot remains uninjured.'

This plan struck Fritz as being so excellent that he set about forming a pot at once with his penknife, but, though he applied himself most energetically to his self-appointed task, he made but slow progress. I showed him a simple way of dividing the fruit by winding a piece of string round it and drawing it so tightly as to cut the gourd in two. By this means we made several basins, which we left in the sun to dry, and which Fritz thought would prove a very welcome addition to his mother's stock of household utensils.

While we marched along we amused ourselves by cutting spoons out of the rind of the gourd, and though the shape of these was rather peculiar, they were a great improvement on the mussel shells that we had been so glad to use on the previous day.

After having advanced for about four hours, we reached a narrow point of land that stretched far out into the sea. At the furthest end of this a hill rose to a considerable eminence. This we climbed with some difficulty, and looked round in the hope that we might perceive some trace of the com-panions we sought.

Once, indeed, I thought our hopes were about to be realized when Fritz, who had already descended the hill, called to me that he had just distinguished a number of human forms along the shore, but that on seeing him they had disappeared quickly behind a projecting rock. It seemed to me hardly likely that our companions would flee from us; however, to satisfy all doubts, we set off in search of the supposed fugitives, but no trace of them was to be seen.

'I am afraid, Fritz,' I said, 'that God, for some wise purpose, no doubt, has decided that we must spend our lives here in exile. I see no prospect of ever getting off this island.'

'Well,' he replied encouragingly, 'it is not such a bad place after all, and I see no reason why, when we are all together, we should not be as happy here as elsewhere.'

His hopeful view of things made me rather ashamed of my own down-heartedness, and as we proceeded on our journey I strove to be as cheerful as possible.

We next turned our steps to a small palm-tree grove which looked most cool and inviting, and which we thought would be much pleasanter to traverse than the open pathway.

While advancing towards it, I was surprised to see a glutinous substance oozing from the end of a reed I had just cut, and, placing my lips to it, I was delighted to find that it was sugar-cane. Here was another of our wants supplied! This discovery seemed to Fritz the most delightful of all. Having cut a little hole, by my directions, in the side of a rod, he fell to sucking the juice with great avidity, but paused now and again to comment on the pleasure which was in

store for his brothers, who, he felt sure, would rejoice equally with himself over the new-found luxury. Then he cut a bundle of the canes, and having stripped them of their leaves, took up his burden and hastened towards the palm grove, where he lay down to rest and eat some of the provisions with which my wife had supplied us before we left.

We had scarcely sat down, however, when our attention was arrested by loud cries, and on looking round we saw a troop of monkeys – which had been alarmed by our appearance and by the barking of Topsy – springing up the trees with wonderful rapidity. Here they felt secure from attack, and proceeded to chatter and grin horribly at us, as if to show their dissatisfaction at our approach.

Seeing that the trees in which they had taken refuge were cocoa palms, it occurred to me that even the temper of the monkeys might be made to serve us; so I told Fritz to treat them to a shower of small stones. Not understanding my motive, he brought his gun to his shoulder, and said he could kill them much more easily with it; but I stopped his purpose instantly.

'It is very wrong, my son,' I said, 'to kill any animal without necessity. These monkeys are doing us no harm, and may be very useful to us if you do as I tell you.'

Abashed by my reproof, he began to pelt the animals with stones, and was greatly astonished at the energy with which they defended themselves, as, plucking the cocoa-nuts, they threw them angrily down on us. This was just what I wanted,

and soon Fritz and I were refreshing ourselves with the milk
of the fruit, which proved to be a most delicious drink. After
having regaled ourselves to our satisfaction – thanks to the
monkeys – we tied together a few of the cocoa-nuts that had
stalks, and, having slung them over my shoulder, proceeded
on our homeward journey.

We had not advanced far when Fritz began to show signs
of fatigue; his burden proved heavier than he had anticipated, and he commenced to think that, after all, his
brothers might not relish the canes as much as he had at first
supposed, and that he had better not carry them farther.
Seeing their weight was really too much for him, I relieved
him of them. My act discomfited him greatly, and made him
feel as if he were of little use to me.

'I fear, father, I have been a hindrance rather than a help
to you today,' he said; 'and I'm sure those at home will say
that I turned my chance to little account when all I could
bring them was a little cocoa-nut milk.'

'Not so, my boy,' I answered him. 'You have been of great
service to me; you have nothing to reproach yourself with on
that score. I fear, however, that the cocoa-nut milk will not
be considered much of a treat. When removed from the shell
it very soon becomes sour, and I should not wonder if what
you have is already vinegar. Let me see in what stage it is.'

Pulling a small flask filled with the liquid from his pocket,
he was about to remove the cord, when it flew out with a pop,
and the liquor foamed like champagne. We tasted it and

found it very agreeable. Fritz felt thoroughly pleased with his manufacture of the new beverage, and trudged on in high spirits towards the place where we had left our gourd vessels. These we found thoroughly hardened by the sun and fit for use, so, putting them in our bags, we hurried on, anxious to reach home before sunset.

We had scarcely got half-way through the wood in which we had breakfasted, when our attention was drawn to Topsy, who rushed past us, barking furiously. Hastening to see the cause of her excitement, we found her in full chase after another troop of monkeys, which her sudden appearance had greatly alarmed.

All managed to get out of her reach, however, except one, which she hemmed in completely; and before we could prevent her, she had killed the poor animal, and had already begun her sanguinary repast. Fritz sprang forward in the hope that he might be in time to save its life; but as he was passing under a tree in which several monkeys sat grinding their teeth and watching with impotent rage the death of their companion, one of them bounded on his shoulder, and, clutching him tightly by the hair, tore and scratched him most unmercifully, but yet clung so fast that no efforts of his own could set him free from his unwelcome assailant.

Going up to them I endeavoured gently to disengage it, and at last succeeded, but not before it was as completely terrified as was Fritz.

Notwithstanding the fright he had met with, he was most

anxious to retain the little creature, and, though I by no means desired to add another to our number under present circumstances, I could not resist his importunity.

'Please, father, let me keep it,' he pleaded. 'I can feed it with nuts and other things which we can easily find, and it will be sure to die if we abandon it.'

'Very well, my son,' I replied, 'you may make a pet of it, but take good care that Topsy's partiality for such animals, which she just now displayed so cruelly, does not deprive you of it.'

Assuring me that he would take good care that no evil should befall it, he placed it on his shoulder and continued on his way. The little monkey, unaccustomed to such a mode of progress, became after a while quite restless and troublesome, so his master's inventive genius was called into play.

Taking a strong cord from his pocket he tied it round the

dog's neck, and setting the new pet on her back, where it seemed quite at ease, he gave it the cord in its paw, and by threats and caresses compelled Topsy to march along peacefully. Our appearance tickled me greatly. 'Don't we seem like a couple of mountebanks on our way to a fair, with our basins and sticks and animals?' I asked. 'Your mother and brothers will be struck with our comical aspect when we reach home.'

'Doubtless they will,' he answered, 'but they will also be delighted to see us safely back, and to know what a good journey we have made. Mother will like the spoons and bowls, I am sure, but Jack will prefer the monkey, for he will find in it a companion who will play as many tricks and be as great a hand at grimaces as himself.'

We now heard the welcoming bark of Bill, and, warned of our approach, the dear ones rushed out to greet us. Everything which we had brought received its share of admiration and welcome; but on the monkey three pairs of bright eyes gazed fixedly. 'Oh, where did you get it?' 'What a pretty creature!' 'Do let me have it just for a moment!' the boys chorused. I answered their questions as well as possible, and then proceeded to show them our other discoveries.

'Why did you bring such a big bundle of sticks?' asked Jack. 'There are plenty like these quite near our tent, and it must have tired you greatly to carry them so far.'

'The burden was certainly rather a heavy one,' I replied, 'but I think it will repay me for my trouble. These are not common rods, but specimens of the sugar-cane, of which you have often heard, and which you can now taste for the first time.'

On hearing this, Jack stuck the end of one of the sticks, in which I had already cut a vent-hole, in his mouth, and uttered a cry of delight.

'Oh, Franz, do taste it! It is just like real sugar! Where did you get them? And are there plenty more?'

I told him that the supply was almost unlimited on the other side of the river; and then I explained the manner of extracting the juice from them. This is done by cutting a small hole in the cane just above the first knot below the end which is to be placed in the mouth. This provides a passage of air, and there is then no difficulty in sucking the juice from the tube.

My wife, as well as the children, was much pleased with this discovery, as she saw that by it a very useful addition was made to her store of provisions. What gratified her most, however, were the basins, spoons, and pots which Fritz and I had manufactured, and which were actual necessaries.

After having displayed all our wares we proceeded to the tent and noticed with pleasure that preparations had been made for giving us a very substantial repast. On one side of the fire hung, on an improvised spit, several fish of different sorts; on the other, a large goose was slowly roasting; while over the fire bubbled a pot of soup, which sent forth a most tempting odour. My wife, seeing me regarding the fowl somewhat dubiously, informed me that it was not, as I supposed, one of the geese that we had brought with us from the wreck, but a bird which Ernest had that day shot, and which he asserted to be a penguin.

I asked him how he could be positive when he had never seen a similar one, and the young scholar replied, 'Before coming near it at all I knew what it was from its shape, which resembles that of a bottle. Then, on examining it closely, I observed that it had all the peculiarities which are mentioned in natural history as belonging to the penguin. It is web-footed; has a long, narrow beak, curved at the end; short legs, and a strong tail which it uses as a support.'

I praised the boy's intelligent observations, and then, seeing the children's eyes fixed intently on the heap of cocoanuts, I bade Fritz teach them how to open them, and added, 'We must not forget the little monkey who has just been deprived of its mother's care. Had you not better try it with some cocoa-nut milk, till we find more suitable food for it?'

The boys, who had previously offered it everything they could think of without being able to tempt it to eat, were gratified to see that this new dainty was quite to its taste, and their fears of not being able to rear it were banished.

We now received a summons to supper, which we gladly obeyed. Sitting on the ground, and making use of our gourd-rind plates and spoons, we enjoyed a hearty meal. Our newly-manufactured articles were found to answer their purpose admirably, and we determined to furnish ourselves with others of the same as soon as possible.

The sun had by this time almost disappeared, and the succeeding chilliness of the air warned us to seek our beds. These our housekeeper had made much warmer and more comfortable by an additional supply of moss that she had collected during the day.

We had not slept long before I was aroused by an unusual disturbance among the fowls on the top of the tent, and by the barking and whining of Topsy and Bill, who were acting as sentinels outside. Rising quickly and seizing my gun, I advanced cautiously to the door. By the clear light of the moon I could see that our faithful dogs were surrounded by more than a dozen jackals, and that a fierce struggle was going on. Four of the invaders had been already overcome by the superior strength of our brave defenders, but the others were just gathering for a renewed attack when a well-directed shot from Fritz, who had also been awakened by the noise and approached me noiselessly, laid two more of the animals dead, and the others, frightened by the report of the gun, scampered off as fast as they could. The dogs, satisfied with their victory, and regardless of the bonds of relationship, appeased their growing hunger with choice bits of their enemies; and Fritz and I again sought the shelter of the tent, where we slept undisturbed till morning.

CHAPTER II

ADVENTURES AND DISCOVERIES

H OW TO occupy ourselves most usefully during this third day on the island was a subject of grave discussion while we partook of breakfast. The boys were anxious for another day's march in search of a suitable place for encampment, while my wife and I thought it better to repair to the wreck, and bring with us from it whatever we considered would add to our comfort. So it was decided that Fritz and I should set out in our tub to the wreck. The other boys begged eagerly to be allowed to go, but I told them that, in order to bring them plenty of good things, I must have room on the raft for them. Seeing the truth of what I said, they relinquished their desire, and each thought of some special article which he wished us to remember.

'Our biscuits are so hard and dry, father,' said Ernest, 'that they are almost uneatable; if you could bring us a little butter it would improve them greatly.'

'He need not do that,' interrupted Jack, 'for there is a whole cask full of something, which I am sure from the smell is butter, close at hand. I found it on the beach yesterday, but, as it was too heavy for me, I hid it, and forgot all about it. Come now and I'll show you where it is.'

Ernest and he started off, and reappeared in a few minutes, carrying between them a large cask, from which a fatty substance was oozing. After having satisfied ourselves that Jack's nose had not deceived him, we cut a small hole, and extracted as much butter as we needed for present use. Then we toasted some biscuits, buttered them hot, and found that a delicious addition had been made to our store of luxuries.

While we were thus employed the dogs entered, and I saw that they had received some deep and painful cuts in last night's contest. Having washed a piece of butter in fresh water, and thus extracted the salt, my wife anointed their wounds, which evidently afforded them great relief.

'If the poor animals had had on spiked collars they would have served as weapons of defence, and they could not have been so badly wounded,' said Jack; 'and if mamma will help me, I will undertake to make some for them today.'

'With all my heart,' answered his mother, 'but I can't see where the materials are to come from.'

'Leave that to Jack,' I said; 'he knows what he is about.'

The tub-boat was soon ready, and, having taken leave of those who were to remain behind, Fritz and I embarked. Before leaving we had set up a pole, to which we fastened a long strip of canvas. This was to serve as a signal to us; in case of danger my wife was to pull it down and fire a gun three times, while we agreed, should we remain all night on the vessel, to burn lights to show that all was well.

When we had got a little way from the shore, I noticed that a strong current was running in the direction in which we were going, and by means of it we were carried a considerable way without much exertion on our part.

On our appearance on board, the lowing of the cows and bleating of the sheep testified to their satisfaction at seeing us again, and the fresh provender and water with which we took care to supply them immediately were consumed with great avidity. Their immediate wants ministered to, we began to consider what was the most important thing to be done.

'I think,' said Fritz, 'that we had better first look out for a sail for our boat. The current, which aided us so much coming, will be against us returning; and as the boat will be heavily laden, and you will be partly taken up with steering, it would be almost impossible for me to row against it.'

His suggestion appeared to me so sensible that I agreed to it at once. I sought out a broken yard, which was large

enough to serve as a mast, and also a weaker piece to which to
fix our sail, and Fritz nailed a thick plank across one of the
tubs, and made a hole in it into which we might stick the
mast. I then cut a large triangular piece from a roll of canvas
which I found in the hold, and I fastened it to the mast as
well as I could. Two ropes which were attached, one to the
yard and the other to the extremity of the boat, enabled us to
direct the sail at pleasure; while, to finish with, Fritz
mounted a small flag, which he watched floating on the
breeze with delight.

By the time our work was completed, the evening was so
far advanced that we decided to remain where we were till
the morrow, so, hoisting a signal as pre-arranged, we made
those on shore aware of our intention. The remainder of the
day was spent in ransacking the vessel, and replacing the
stones that we had thrown into our boat for ballast by
articles which were likely to prove of infinite value to us
during our exile. Anticipating a lengthened sojourn in this
uninhabited country, I sought out those things which would
help us to sustain life and enable us to protect ourselves from
the attacks of enemies. First of all, we provided ourselves
with a large quantity of powder and lead, knowing that
without these our means of subsistence would be scant; and I
also made myself the possessor of a varied assortment of
kettles, pots, basins, knives, forks, and other domestic utensils, with which the ship was well stocked. Amongst the
captain's private property we found several bottles of wine

and brandy, which, along with a few Westphalian hams and certain sacks of wheat and maize, I transferred to the boat. At the request of Fritz, I added to our already heavy cargo some hammocks and blankets, which he thought would add greatly to our comfort; also some cord, sailcloth, and a keg of sulphur with which to renew our supply of matches. By the time we had got all these stowed away, our tubs were loaded to the edge.

Night fell suddenly, and, as I did not consider it safe to remain on the wreck, we made our preparations for passing the hours of darkness in the tub-boat which was securely anchored close to the vessel.

As soon as day broke I set to work to make arrangements for conveying the cattle to land. This seemed at first somewhat perplexing. Fritz suggested that we should make a raft for them, but I pointed out the difficulty of getting it to land, even if the animals could be got to remain quietly on it, which I very much doubted. At last it occurred to me that a sort of floating apparatus might be attached to each animal, and as the idea was quickly seized by Fritz, who longed for the fun of seeing them in the water, I resolved to try the experiment.

Selecting a sheep, I attached floats to its sides, and, having placed a cord round its neck, I threw it into the water. At first it disappeared, but soon it struggled to the surface, and, supported by the belt, swam excellently. Satisfied of the practicability of the plan, we set to work vigorously, and

proceeded to provide all our livestock with this novel swim-
ming suit. A quantity of cork which we discovered on board
served to keep the smaller animals afloat, but on each side of
the cow and ass it was necessary to fasten an empty cask by
leather bands over their backs. To complete the arrangement, a strong cord was knotted round the neck of each of
them, and with these we intended to tow them after us when
we got on board the boat. This done, we made a breach in the
side of the vessel, and lowered them into the water. At first
they seemed greatly frightened, and plunged so violently
that I feared they would break loose from us, but soon they
resigned themselves to the necessities of the case, and floated
along gallantly. Fritz and I now embarked and sailed
towards land, congratulating ourselves meanwhile on our
manufacture of the sail, which was serving its purpose
admirably.

On our return my wife drew my attention to a belt of
yellow skin which Jack wore, and into which he had thrust
two old pistols.

'Why, Jack, you look exactly like a brigand,' I said.
'Where did you pick up that wonderful adornment?'

'I made it myself,' he answered with apparent satisfaction;
'and I also made a couple of collars for the dogs, which will
enable them to defend themselves.'

Calling Topsy and Bill, he showed me the bands,
bristling with long nails which he had fastened on them.

'Very cleverly done, my boy,' I said approvingly; 'but

where did you get the leather? Surely you did not make that, too!'

'Fritz's jackal furnished me with that,' he replied; 'and mamma sewed the ends together.'

Commending his ingenuity, I betook myself to the tent, where my wife had gone to prepare supper, but, thinking our store of victuals must be very low, I sent Fritz for one of the hams that we had brought with us from the wreck. The children were delighted with the sight of this, which they called 'civilized food', and which, together with some turtle's eggs that Jack had found in the sand by the sea-shore, afforded us a delicious repast. While we were enjoying the good things before us, I asked my wife how she had passed the time during my absence.

'I have many strange adventures and daring deeds to recount,' she answered laughing. 'When you left, I resolved to set off and explore the island, in the hope that before your return I might have discovered some suitable spot to which we could remove our tent. The boys, who entered joyfully into my plan, provided themselves with arms and provisions, and, bearing a can of water and an axe, and accompanied by the dogs, I set out on my march. As the sun was beating down upon us most unmercifully, we hurried our steps towards the little wood on our right; but here, owing to the long grass and weeds which tripped us continually, our progress was exceedingly slow and laborious. For a good while we advanced without seeing anything worthy of

notice, but suddenly we were startled by a loud whirring
noise quite close to us, and at the same moment a huge bird
rose almost at our feet and flew swiftly skywards. The boys
were so taken by surprise that they did not attempt to take
aim. "How unfortunate!" moaned Ernest, as it disappeared.
"A moment more and I should have brought it down."

' "We must just be more watchful again," remarked Jack.
"And now, as the bird is lost to us, the best thing we can do is
to look for its nest, which must be close at hand."

'After searching carefully among the grass and reeds,
Ernest found the nest, but the contents did not repay him for
his trouble; they consisted only of a few broken egg-shells,
which led us to conclude that the young ones had left but a
short time before.

'We then entered a little grove of trees, the height of which
I had never seen equalled; amongst their branches fluttered
immense numbers of birds of varied and beautiful plumage,
who treated us to a concert of most delightful music.

'Ernest found entertaining employment in trying to classify them, but the prodigious height of the trees on which they were perched rendered his effort almost useless. The form and wide girth of these trees astonished us greatly. Their immense trunks, instead of growing out of the ground, were supported by powerful roots, which formed a series of supporting arches immediately under the trunk and thence ran out in all directions, disappearing into the soil only here and there.'

'We could build a grand house in one of the trees which mother has just described,' cried Ernest eagerly.

'Why, Ernest,' I said, 'you don't want to become altogether a fowl of the air, I hope. I think it is wiser to keep on *terra firma* as long as possible. What would your mother say to such a mad freak?'

'I was just about to suggest it,' she answered, 'when Ernest interrupted me. I think the plan a capital one, and I expect when you see the place that you will agree with me.'

Such was my wife's account of the events of the day, and when it was finished we all retired for the night.

The next morning I felt greatly refreshed by the sound sleep which I had enjoyed, and while my wife was preparing breakfast I brought up from the shore the various articles which she had found there the day before. Having stored them in a corner of the tent, I sat down with my family to our morning meal.

'Now, my dear husband, have you been thinking over my grand plan for changing our quarters?' asked my wife, as she placed a steaming bowl of milk before me, which, along with some sailors' biscuits, was to form our repast.

'Yes,' I replied; 'I considered your project very seriously, but to my mind it has several disadvantages. In the first place, here we are close to the wreck, where there are still many things which, if we could obtain them, will be invaluable to us in our exiled state, and which, if we remove farther inland, we must give up all hope of recovering. Besides, this spot is well suited to our defenceless condition. We are shut in between sea and rocks, and it is with difficulty that any enemy can approach us. For these reasons I think it would be foolish to leave it hastily. Now what have you to urge in favour of your plan?'

'I think I can produce as many objections to our remaining here as you can to removing,' she replied smilingly; 'and I expect to have little trouble in bringing you to my way of thinking. Our present habitation may be secure enough, but still our adventure with the jackals proves that it is not unassailable. They managed to find us out, and is it not possible that more cunning and dangerous animals may do the same? In our home in the tree we should feel perfectly secure from the encroachments of such terrible visitors. As regards the treasures still on board the wreck, I would renounce them willingly rather than suffer the anxiety that your absence causes me. Further, here, in this sandy desert, we are exposed during the whole day to the scorching rays of the sun, which the tent is powerless to ward off, and I very much fear the health of the children may suffer in conse-

quence. Think how different it would be if we lived in the
shelter of a cool grove, where the heat could hardly penetrate, and where delicious fruits are hanging on all sides,
inviting us to refresh ourselves.'

'Very well argued,' said I. 'You have almost, if not quite,
convinced me. I shall go to the wood now, and if the tree be as
suitable for habitation as your description leads me to think
it is, we shall lose no time in transporting our possessions
thither.'

Setting out, I reached without adventure the much talked-
of plantation, and was in no wise disappointed in the beauty
of the spot. The size of the trees surpassed anything I could
have imagined, and seemed admirably adapted for our purpose. I immediately decided to put my wife's plan into
execution, and on reaching home congratulated her heartily
on her selection of such a charming spot for our future abode.
The boys wished to start on the moment, and it was with
difficulty that I could get them to listen to me while I
explained the different arrangements which must be made
before we could transport our belongings to the other side of
the river.

My wife thought the cow and ass could carry them, but
when I told her how necessary it was that our provisions and
ammunition should be conveyed without risk of wetting, she
at once agreed with me that our best plan was to construct a
bridge, which would enable us easily to get all in safety to the
other side.

In order to carry out this plan, however, a lot of timber

must be procured, and for this it was necessary to take another voyage to the wreck. We soon got ready our tub-boat and I, accompanied this time by both Ernest and Fritz, set out on our second journey by sea. Again wind and tide were in our favour, and we floated swiftly along. As we were passing close to a small island that lay out in the bay, Ernest, who was amusing himself with the telescope, suddenly cried, 'Look, papa! Did ever you see such a flock of birds?' and a cloud of sea-mews, albatrosses, and other members of the feathered tribe, rose, wheeled their flight in ever-returning circles, and settled again on the shore, all the time uttering most ear-piercing cries.

'There must be some cause for such an assemblage,' said I. 'We had better approach, and see what has attracted them in such numbers.'

We had not advanced much nearer before we could dis-tinguish a dark object which lay half covered by the water, and on which a countless host of birds was feasting ravenously.

'It is the carcass of one of those sea-monsters of which we have often read, and which are sure to abound here,' said Ernest, who dearly liked to give his opinion on all subjects, and who, this time, was not mistaken.

It was the dead body of a huge shark on which the birds were perched.

'What a gigantic brute!' said Fritz, as he regarded it wonderingly. 'From what I have read of sharks I had no idea

of their size. Why, our donkey would only be a bite to such a monster as this!'

'It is the largest I have ever seen,' I replied.

Wishing to examine the carcass minutely, Ernest frightened away the birds which still hovered around it. We then cut off some portions of the rough skin, which, it occurred to me, might be useful in various ways, especially as a substitute for a file. These Jack nailed on a piece of plank to dry, and we returned to the boat.

When about to put out to sea again to go to the wreck, I noticed a large number of planks and beams that the tide had cast upon the shore of the island. These I saw with extreme pleasure, for they were well adapted for the purpose I had in view, and would save us the trouble of taking a longer journey.

Having selected a good many of the most suitable, and bound them together into a sort of raft, which we secured to the stern of our boat, we hoisted our sail and turned our faces homeward.

We soon arrived at our landing-place, and were received with a joyful shout by Jack and Franz, who, along with their mother, were wandering by the bank of the river, and were greatly astonished at our speedy return. Jack had a fishing-net slung over his shoulder, and little Franz dangled a carefully-tied handkerchief, whose contents seemed to afford him extreme satisfaction.

'What treasure have you got there, my son?' I asked,

seeing that he expected me to be interested in his possessions.

'Ever so many crabs, papa,' he answered gleefully; 'and I caught them every one myself.'

Here he opened his handkerchief and displayed a good number of craw-fish, which he had found sticking to the remains of one of the jackals that had assailed us, and that we had thrown into the river. Jack's net also contained many of these small shell-fish, but, as they were very young, I begged the boys to replace them in the water, in order that they might grow larger, and serve us as an article of food. This they obediently did, though I saw that Franz relinquished his with very evident regret. In order to divert his attention from what he looked on as a great loss, I asked him if he could point out to me any place which had struck his fancy as a site for the bridge. But before he had time to answer, Ernest called:

'I know a splendid place quite near here. If you come I will show it to you, and you will be sure to choose it.'

I followed him to the spot that had met with his approval, and found that it was indeed very suitable, the only objection to it being that it was a considerable distance from the nearest point where we could land the timber. This difficulty was overcome, however, by imagining our cow a reindeer, and adopting the custom of the Laplanders. Taking a strong rope, I fastened it round a piece of timber, and then tied the other end to the horns of the animal, which I drove forward. Thus by degrees our wood was removed to the chosen spot.

'Now,' said I, when everything was ready to commence operations, 'we must measure the width of the stream, as we may not have any logs long enough to reach across.'

'That will be easy enough,' said Fritz. 'It will only be necessary to tie a stone to the end of a cord and throw it across. We can then draw it close to the edge of the water on the other side, and the length of the twine will give us the measure we seek.'

Having put this ingenious yet simple plan into practice, we found that the river was about eighteen feet wide. As it required the principal beams to have a resting-place on each bank of the stream, we selected three, each of which was about twenty-four feet in length; but how to lay these enormous pieces of wood across was a startling difficulty, which we discussed for a long time without hitting on any way of solving it. At last a means of accomplishing our desire struck me. Taking a strong rope, I tied the end of one of the beams to the branch of a tree that overshadowed us; then I fastened a longer rope to the other end of the beam, and, walking boldly through the river, carried it to the opposite shore, where I threw it over another branch. Coming back, I attached the other end of this second rope to the cow and ass, and drove them rapidly from the shore. My plan succeeded admirably. The log rose slowly in the air, and swung to the other side of the river amid the shouts of the boys, its own weight keeping it firm.

The task which we had now to accomplish was compara-tively easy. Two other similar logs were laid parallel with the

first, and a series of short planks was nailed across them. Thus we constructed a bridge which was between eight and nine feet in width. By the time this was completed night had again closed in around us, and we returned to our tent.

Since the night of our attack by the jackals, I was continually in fear of the encroachment of some new enemy, and I spent many sleepless hours in expectation of a warning bark from the dogs, on whose watchfulness I fully depended. This night especially sleep refused to visit my eyelids, and I tossed restlessly on my mossy bed, longing for the dawn. Suddenly my ear caught a sound outside the tent, and, while listening for it to be repeated, I heard a low whine from one of the dogs. This was succeeded by a loud bark, so I sprang up quickly, fearing there was some cause for alarm. Advancing to the tent-door, I opened it cautiously and peered out into the night. The moon was now hidden behind a heavy bank of clouds, and I could distinguish nothing but Topsy and Bill, who jumped round me with every appearance of terror.

Expecting the approach of some enemy, I re-entered the tent and awoke my family. 'There is danger of some sort close at hand,' I said, 'and we must be prepared to meet it. Rise quickly, and get ready our fire-arms. Keep close to me, and take good care not to go a foot from our dwelling. It may be savages from some neighbouring island, who have come to try their arrows on the white skins; but whatever it be, man or beast, let us be ready to receive it.'

While the boys were making their hurried preparations, the dogs continued to bark loudly, and even the monkey, as if it scented danger in the air, became restless, and burrowed deeper into its nest of hay, as if in search of greater security. When all were ready, I opened the door carefully. Scarcely had I done so when the dogs rushed past me and cowered trembling in a corner of the tent. Whatever the danger might be, it was evidently close at hand, so I called the boys to remain near me, while I withdrew to the outside. The moon, which, until now, had been almost completely hidden, emerged at this moment from behind its veil of cloud, and shone down brightly, displaying the horrible grinning faces and glittering lances of about a dozen savages, who stood within a few yards of us. Seeing that they were discovered, they raised a wild yell and rushed towards the tent, but not before we were prepared for their attack.

'Now, boys,' I called to the boys, who stood behind me; 'here they come. Better to frighten than hurt them, if we can, so aim above their heads. Fire!'

Our reception of them was even more effective than I

expected. For a moment they stood paralysed, as if the earth had opened in front of them; then, uttering a demoniac shriek of disappointment and terror, they turned and fled with wonderful rapidity towards the sea.

They plunged into the water, and struck out boldly for a small island that lay in the middle of the bay. We waited, hoping to see them arrive at their destination, but the light of the moon was not strong enough to admit of this; so, firing another volley as a farewell, which this time they received in silence, we hurried towards the tent.

At daybreak we got up, and set about our preparations for removing as quickly as possible to the Promised Land, as the children had named that part of the island where we intended to take up our abode.

CHAPTER III

THE HOUSE IN THE TREE

BREAKFAST AT an end, we prepared to set out. My wife produced several sacks that she had very cleverly made out of a piece of sailcloth, and having placed them as panniers on the ass and cow, filled them with such articles as were likely to be most useful to us. Our cooking utensils, hammocks, and blankets were all carefully packed into them, and we did not forget to provide ourselves with a good store of butter, cheese, biscuits, and other articles of food. Before we had finished loading the animals, my wife begged me to reserve a little corner for Franz, who could not possibly walk the whole distance, as well as room for the fowls, which, she said, it was most important we should take with us. I gave in to her desire, and made a comfortable seat for the little fellow between the panniers on the donkey's back, and Ernest and Fritz set off in hot pursuit of the fowls and pigeons. They returned in a few minutes, minus the objects of their chase, having only succeeded in putting themselves in a bad temper. My wife had watched their vain efforts with amusement, and told them she would undertake to catch all the birds without any trouble whatever. At this they looked slightly incredulous, and asked laughingly if she thought she could run faster than they.

'I don't mean to run after them at all,' was her reply; 'but I shall adopt a much better plan, as you will be obliged to admit.'

Upon that, taking a few handfuls of grain out of a small bag, she scattered some of it on the ground, and soon the whole feathered flock cackled and cooed around her. By this means she decoyed them into the tent, and I shut it from the outside, thus making them fast prisoners. With wings and feet tied, we placed them in two hampers on each side of the donkey, and covered them with a cloth, so that, hidden from the heat of the sun, they might not disturb us by their cackling.

All those possessions which we could not carry with us we stored away in the tent, and having secured it as carefully as possible, and placed all our large casks, both full and empty, around it, I gave the signal for departure. At the head of the procession marched Fritz, looking very important, with his gun on his shoulder and his game-bag slung by his side. Directly after him came my wife, leading the cow and ass; on the latter little Franz was seated proudly, and evidently delighted with this, to him, new form of locomotion. Now and again, however, terror overcame him for a moment, and his mother had to hasten to the rescue, and hold him firmly until he had regained his courage, when he would tell her to go away and leave him to himself, as he was not a bit afraid. The goats, driven by Jack, formed the third division of our caravan; next came Ernest and the sheep; I myself, accompanied by Bill, formed the rear-guard; while Topsy, looking most grotesque with the monkey on her back, ran here, there, and everywhere, as if excited by her load, sniffing and barking, and constantly on the alert.

As we approached the bridge, the sow, which we could not prevail on to accompany the party at first, rejoined us; but her short grunts testified that she regarded our proceeding with anything but satisfaction.

The crossing of the river was effected without accident. Once arrived at the other side, however, we were beset by new difficulties. The rich pasture proved a temptation to the cattle that they were powerless to resist, and all our efforts to urge them forward were for a long time useless. Had it not been for the dogs, who materially helped us, we should never have succeeded in gathering together our wandering flock. In order to avoid further delay of a similar description, I directed our leader to take the way along the coast, as there was no pasture there to cause the animals to loiter, and besides it would be a much less troublesome road for ourselves to traverse. We concluded our journey without further adventure, reaching the spot chosen by my wife for our future home.

After we had halted, our primary duty was to unload the beasts of burden, and turn them out to feed, first taking care to tie their forefeet loosely together, so that they might not stray away. The hens and pigeons were then allowed to regain their freedom, and were left to wander at their own

discretion, and my wife and I sat down on the soft grass with which the soil was carpeted, and took counsel together regarding the construction of our future habitation. The chief difficulty that presented itself was the formation of a staircase by which to mount to our airy abode, and we were engaged in a lengthy discussion of this matter when we were disturbed by hearing two shots fired in succession at a short distance from us, and immediately after Fritz's voice crying excitedly, 'Hit! Hit!' In a few minutes he made his appearance, carrying by the hind legs a tigercat, on which both his shots had taken effect, and which he held proudly up to us to examine.

'Well done, Fritz,' said I. 'You have rendered good service not only to the fowls and pigeons, amongst which this rascal would have made sad havoc, but also to the cattle, on whose account we should have good cause to fear its presence in our vicinity. To such robbers we must show no quarter, or the consequences to our livestock will be most deplorable.'

'What will be done with its skin?' asked Jack, as he stroked its beautiful coat admiringly.

'I should like part of it to make a hunting-belt in which to carry my knife and pistols,' replied Fritz.

'As the prize is yours, your desire must certainly be gratified; and I think the tail would answer that purpose admirably,' I remarked. 'The skin of the body and legs would make good cases to contain the pieces of plate which we found in the captain's cabin.'

I showed Fritz how to flay the tigercat, and then put aside the meat for salting and storing.

Meanwhile Ernest was searching for some large flat stones with which to construct a fireplace, and Franz was industriously gathering a bundle of dry sticks for a fire by which to cook our evening meal. The latter soon made his appearance, puffing under a heavy load of branches, and munching something with evident satisfaction. Fancying it might be some fruit of a poisonous nature which, in his ignorance, he was devouring, his mother called to him to throw it down immediately; but her fears were set at rest when he held out for our inspection a few figs that he had found on one of the neighbouring trees.

'I knew at once what they were,' he said, in reply to his mother's eager questioning, 'for I remembered the fig-tree that grew in our own garden in Switzerland, and I saw that the one from which I plucked these was exactly the same.'

'Fortunately, there is no harm done this time, Franz,' I

remarked; 'but in the future you must be very cautious about what you put into your mouth. Many fruits which have a very tempting exterior, and which are even delicious to the taste, contain a large amount of poison, and such it is impossible for you to recognize. By consulting the monkey, however, you will always be able to decide what is fit for eating and what is not, for its instinct enables it to distinguish between those things which are suitable for food and those which are not.'

Hardly had I said these words when Franz ran to the monkey, which was perched on a low branch of one of the adjacent trees, and offered it some of the figs with which his pockets were filled. The animal, after having sniffed and examined them on all sides, at length began to eat them, and showed appreciation of the delicacy by making all sorts of droll grimaces. Seeing that the fruit was thoroughly approved of by our 'foretaster', the boys ran off in search of some more.

The boys had not yet returned from their search after figs when supper was ready, and I was about to set out after them when I heard a startled cry; rushing in the direction from which it proceeded, I saw a large cobra, one of the most beautiful, though most dangerous, of all reptiles, winding its way through the tangled grass. As with head erect and forked tongue extended it approached the alarmed group, Fritz, whose presence of mind rarely forsook him, hit it a heavy blow on the head with his gun, and so well directed was the stroke that in a few minutes it lay dead at our feet. As if to avenge himself for the alarm which it had caused us, Jack advanced, and, imitating the superstitious conduct of the Indians, cut off its head and tail, and carried them home as a trophy.

This incident increased our anxiety to take up our abode in the tree as soon as we could, but, as the evening was pretty far advanced, it was impossible to have our arrangements completed before nightfall. We therefore decided to make the best possible use of the hour of daylight that remained to us, and provide ourselves with a shelter from the dew and insects. This we did by suspending our hammocks from the arched roots of the tree, and covering the whole with sail-cloth. When the preparation for our comfort and safety during the night was finished, I went down to the beach with Fritz and Ernest, where I expected to find some pieces of wood that would serve as the steps of a ladder which I intended to construct. There was plenty of timber to be had, but the logs were all so large, and would have been so troublesome to cut to the proper size, that I decided to go elsewhere in search of something more suitable. We were about to retire from the spot when Ernest attracted my attention to a quantity of bamboos that grew half-buried in the sand. Some of these we pulled, and found that, when cleaned and stripped of their leaves, they would form admirable ladder steps. With my axe I cut a lot of them into lengths of three or four feet, and tied them in three bundles, one of which each of us slung over his shoulder.

Seeing at no great distance a thick bed of reeds, I directed

my steps towards it in order to cut some, that I might use the
hard ends as heads to my arrows. We were approaching with
that caution which past experience had taught us to use
when treading on unknown ground, when Topsy rushed past
us like a mad thing, and immediately a large flock of flam-
ingoes rose and flew off with extreme swiftness. Fritz, who
was always on his guard, had just time to level his gun and
fire before they were out of range. Two of the birds fell, one
quite dead, the other only slightly wounded in the wing. The
latter made use of its long legs, which gave it the appearance
of being mounted on stilts, and, hurrying through marsh and
reeds, would probably have made its escape had not Bill
bounded off in pursuit. The dog soon overtook it, and,
seizing it by the wing, held it till I came to the rescue. Fritz
was wild with delight at the idea of possessing this strange

creature alive, and turned his attention to examining its wounds, which he was happy to see were very trifling.

'It will make an attractive addition to our poultry yard when I get it tamed,' he said. 'Look at its splendid plumage! I never saw anything like it. But, as well as being beautiful, it is also very curious. Though it has long legs like the stork, which enable it to run quickly, it is web-footed like a goose, so that it is as much at home on sea as on land.'

While he was finding out the many peculiarities of this strange bird, I set about cutting a number of the coveted reeds, and, this done, we took up our burdens and returned to our family. Jack and Franz were delighted with the new addition to our livestock, but their feelings were not participated in by their mother, who saw in the bird only another mouth to feed. On this point I did not share her anxiety, as I felt sure our new guest would provide itself with food from the river, and I set myself to dress its wounds with an ointment compounded of butter and wine.

While I was occupied in my surgical operation, the youngsters had tied several reeds together, and were endeavouring to measure the height of one of the large trees; but they soon relinquished the effort, and came to me to announce the impossibility of reaching even the lowest branches. I told them that I had a plan for overcoming the difficulty, which, if they had patience for a little, they would see me carrying out. First, I constructed a bow by taking a bamboo cane and drawing it into an arch with a piece of cord;

then, having pointed several reeds at one end, I garnished
the other with feathers taken from the dead flamingo, and
weighted the arrow thus formed by filling the hollow reed
with sand. The boys were not long in finding out what I was
doing, and crowded round me shouting joyously, 'A bow and
arrows! Oh, papa, for which of us have you made them? Do
let me have a shot!'

'Patience, my dear children,' I said, in reply. 'This is not a
toy, but an article which will, I expect, be very useful. If you
are quiet for an instant, you will see what I intend to do with
it.'

Taking the end of a ball of cotton with which my wife
supplied me, I fastened it to one of the arrows, and having
unwound it, I shot the arrow so that it passed over one of the
stoutest branches and fell on the other side, carrying the
thread with it. By measuring the half of the cotton it was
now easy enough to calculate the height of our proposed
dwelling, and to judge what length of ladder it would be
necessary to make. These preliminary steps taken, we set
about the construction of our flight of steps, which we found
must be forty feet long. I measured off about a hundred feet
of strong rope. This I divided into two parts, and laid on the
grass. I then told Fritz to saw the bamboos into lengths of
two feet each, and, aided by Ernest, I fastened these by both
ends to the ropes, at intervals of about twelve inches. Jack
completed the job by driving a stout nail through each piece
of wood, and into the rope, so as effectually to prevent them

from shifting. We then shot the end of the rope over the branch as we had previously done, and drew the ladder up without difficulty. Afterwards we fastened the lower cord to one of the roots of the mangrove, and our stairs were ready for use.

Each of the boys was anxious to be the first to test its strength, but as Jack's nimbleness was in his favour, I told him to lead the way. He instantly commenced his ascent, and in a few minutes reached the first branch. Fritz was the next to mount, and taking a hammer and some nails with him, he secured the ladder so firmly to the tree that I had no hesitation in hazarding the ascent myself. Arrived safely at the top, I found that everything equalled our highest expectation, and I felt sure that a most safe and comfortable dwelling might be established there. Before descending, I managed to attach a large pulley to one of the branches, by means of which we could easily raise the timber that would be necessary to form the ground-work of our habitation. While I was so employed night fell suddenly, and I had to complete the fixture by the light of the moon. Having called the boys, who were clambering in all directions, we descended together; and while waiting for supper, which my wife was busily preparing, we collected a quantity of dry branches, twigs, and grass, and heaped them up close to the spot that we had chosen for our temporary encampment.

Supper taken and our evening prayer offered, my wife and children were soon resting in their hammocks, which swung from the overhanging roots, and I arranged the collected fuel in a circle round the tree and set it on fire. Owing to our close proximity to a large forest, I had no doubt but that many fierce animals were in the vicinity. I therefore resolved to watch till morning, and keep the fire burning as the most effective means of warding off a midnight attack. During the night I was in a continual state of alarm, and even my wife failed to obtain the sleep she sought. Every minute some new noise startled us – the whole air appeared filled with dismal sounds; now it seemed the sullen roar of some irritated animal in the distance – again an angry howl that sounded just beside us. Even the very trees added their mite to the general confusion, and rustled and crackled as if under some heavy weight.

Now, for the first time, my wife began to regret our change of locality, as she thought of the comparative tranquillity which reigned around our former habitation. I tried to still her anxiety by telling her that next night we should be safely lodged; but at the same time my own heart was filled with fear, and I longed for the light of day. Very slowly did the hours pass, but by degrees the strange noises decreased; only now and again the loud roar of some king of the forest, before whom the smaller animals fled in silence, reached our ears. Sleep now began to assert its domination, and I entertained the hope that even yet my wife might be able to secure a few hours of sound repose. I covered her carefully with blankets, and also wrapped one round myself; for, notwithstanding the

fire that was still burning brightly, the air was very chill. I then sat down on the grass, and my thoughts reverted longingly to our peaceful home in the lovely Swiss valley, which, in all probability, we should never see again.

Suddenly a loud howl of agony, in our immediate neighbourhood, roused me from my reverie, and the others from their slumbers. My wife and children started from their hammocks, half asleep, and hardly knowing how they had been awakened. Taking up my gun, I advanced beyond the fiery circle, and the boys, encouraged by my example, followed me closely. Before we had gone many steps we were able to distinguish the cause of our disturbance. Hanging by its tail to the branch of a tree was a mighty serpent, its body coiled round a large tiger that had been unwary enough to come within its reach, and that had paid for his daring with his life. A bloody contest must have preceded the victory, for on each of the combatants cruel wounds had been inflicted.

For a moment we stood motionless regarding this wonderful spectacle; then Bill, who had no idea of playing an inactive part in the adventure, rushed boldly to the attack. I called and whistled on him to return, but in his excitement my signs were unheeded. Knowing what his fate was sure to be, I seized the gun, which, with wise foresight, Ernest had brought with him, and aiming at the snake, that was just in the act of turning its deadly fangs on its new assailant, I fired, and my ball took deadly effect. Gradually the reptile's hold on its victim relaxed; its long body hung for a moment trembling in the air; then its tail unwound itself from the branch, and the monster fell heavily to the ground. On examining it, I found it to be a boa-constrictor of more than eighteen feet in length. When I explained to the children what a dangerous creature it was, they rejoiced greatly that even one such had been removed from our path.

'What a pity we cannot turn it to any account!' said Ernest, who was rapidly being taught by circumstances to utilize everything that came in his way.

'I did not say that we could not; and I am happy to tell you that its skin will be most valuable to us for making shoes, of which we shall soon all have need,' I retorted.

Having skinned it, I turned my attention to its prey, which I found to be that most bloodthirsty of all beasts, the royal tiger. It also we robbed of its beautiful coat, and left its flesh for the dogs to feast on.

By this time day had dawned. As soon as breakfast was over, my wife harnessed our beasts of burden with the straps which, under my directions, she had made on the previous day, and started with the three younger boys to the beach for a supply of driftwood. While they were away on this expedition, Fritz and I mounted the tree and set to work to hew down useless branches that might impede our progress. Above those which were to serve as joists for our flooring we allowed a few to remain at a height of about eight feet, and on these we intended to hang our hammocks. A little higher up a few others were so trimmed as to form rafters for the support

of the roof, which, for the present, was to consist of a
sailcloth. A space was thus cleared away, wide enough to
afford sufficient room for our dwelling.

Meantime a large quantity of timber had been dragged
from the shore, and the necessary beams and planks were
with little difficulty raised to their places with the help of the
pulley. By midday the floor was laid, and surrounded with a
solid handrail to prevent accidents. Nothing remained to be
done but to put on the roof and raise the hammocks; but this
my wife positively forbade us to commence till we had
partaken of a light luncheon.

'A hungry man's work is no work,' she said, as she laid
before us a large pile of biscuits and some fresh warm milk,
with which we regaled ourselves to her and our own satisfaction. Then we spread the sailcloth over the high branches,
and, having drawn it down on both sides, nailed it securely to
the handrail, so that, as the huge trunk of the tree formed a
protection at the back, we were thoroughly sheltered on
three sides. The fourth, which faced the sea, was left open for
the present, but I hit upon a plan for closing it in case of need.
This was to nail another sailcloth to a roller, so that we could
raise or lower it at will, like a blind. When we had slung our
hammocks on the branches that had been left for that
purpose, our 'Nest', as Jack baptized the aerial structure,
was built, and we could look forward to a night of undisturbed repose, such as we had not enjoyed since the storm
which wrecked our little schooner had arisen. Some portion

of the day being still before us, we continued our carpenter work, and from the remainder of the wood constructed a table and a few benches, which we fixed between the large roots of the trees. In this outdoor dining-room we looked forward to spending many pleasant hours. We also erected a small stable at the foot of the ladder, which we intended for the accommodation of all our livestock, except the hens. They had followed their natural instinct, and had sought out a peaceful roosting-place amongst the branches of our tree.

My wife now prepared to dish up our supper, which consisted of a stew that she had made from the flamingo shot the previous day, and which we unanimously pronounced to be delicious. This repast despatched, we closed the animals in their shed, and began our ascent to the 'Nest'.

Our minds undisturbed by thoughts of danger, we soon fell asleep, and the night passed by in sweet tranquillity.

CHAPTER IV

RETURN TO TENT HOUSE

NEXT MORNING we were awakened by the joyous twittering of the birds that seemed to people in hundreds the branches overhead.

I proposed that we should amuse ourselves by giving names to those parts of the island with which we were already acquainted. 'If we do this we shall be much better able to understand each other's references.'

'What a grand idea!' cried all the children at once. 'Let us invent words on the spot. Where shall we begin?'

'Naturally at the first point of land which we touched,' I responded, 'the bay where we found a welcome shelter.'

'I think Lobster Creek would be a good name,' said Jack, 'since it was there that one of them caught me by the leg.'

'No, no,' interrupted his mother, 'rather call it the Creek of Tears, seeing that in your terror you shed so many on that occasion.'

At this remark, which rendered Jack decidedly uncomfortable, his brothers set up a shout of laughter; but I cut it short by giving it as my opinion that, in gratitude to God, we ought to christen the spot in question Deliverance Bay. This choice gave universal satisfaction, and was unanimously adopted. All the points in our territory then received names in succession. The site of our first encampment was called Tent House; the island opposite it Shark Island, in memory of Fritz's adventure with the sea monster; the swamp where we had supplied ourselves with reeds, Flamingo Marsh; the eminence on which we had mounted to look for our lost companions, the Hill of Disappointment; while our present abode retained the name of The Nest, which had already been conferred on it. I suggested a slight alteration, however, and proposed to call it Falcon's Nest, 'for,' as I said to the children, 'you are bold and daring like young falcons, and ever on the look-out for prey.'

On the following day it was decided to go to Tent House, in order to renew our supply of ammunition, and also to provide ourselves with a further stock of provisions. Ernest urged us to bring back the geese and ducks with us, as they could find in the vicinity of our abode a stream well suited to their habits. This time we agreed to take a path which we had not before traversed, and having barricaded the door and windows of the 'Nest', we soon were on our way.

Coasting the stream we fell into a most agreeable route, under the shade of some large trees. The boys ran on before, wandering now to the right, now to the left, and sometimes making me anxious by disappearing altogether from view. When we reached the end of the grove I thought it right to summon them together, but before I had time to do so Ernest came running towards me at the top of his speed, and

I could scarcely believe my ears when I heard him shouting gleefully, 'Potatoes, father; I have found some potatoes!' I was slow to think that he had really made this most useful discovery, and I followed doubtingly to the spot where he told me they grew. What was my joy to find that his announcement was correct, and that a large area was covered with this most valuable plant!

When I told the boys that it was without doubt potatoes that were growing here so plentifully, they set up a shout of delight; and Jack instantly threw himself on the ground and commenced grubbing up the earth to get at the roots. 'Though Ernest made the discovery, I shall be the first to supply you with some of the potatoes,' he said, as he worked away with great zeal. 'Nip,' as the boys had christened the monkey, failed not to imitate his master's example, and in a few minutes they brought to light between them a large quantity of the excellent fruit. These were stowed away in our game-bags, and we resumed our journey, determined to return on a later day to complete the harvest.

Discoursing on the wonders which we had that day seen for the first time, we arrived at Jackal River, as we had called it. This we crossed without any difficulty, and after a few minutes' walk arrived at Tent House, where we found everything as we had left it. Our fears that the savages might have returned and deprived us of the goods that we had collected with so much difficulty were happily groundless. We set to work immediately to gather those things which we looked upon as most necessary. I helped my wife to open the butter cask from which she wished to fill her jar. Ernest collected the needful supply of powder and shot, while Fritz and Jack endeavoured to catch the geese and ducks, which were floating about on the water, and which would not allow themselves to be approached. The boys were at last obliged to resort to stratagem, so, tying a bit of cheese to a long string, they threw it into the river. The greedy birds were soon attracted by the bait, which they swallowed voraciously, and Fritz had then no difficulty in drawing them to land. By repeating the manoeuvre he soon made himself master of all the rebels. He then cut off the string close to the beak, and left them to digest the rest as well as they could. Each of the prisoners was afterwards tied up securely in a piece of sail-cloth and placed in one of the game bags. It was important that we should not return to the 'Nest' without some salt,

but as we were already pretty heavily laden, we were obliged to make a limited quantity suffice. This we found amongst the rocks, and threw into the potato bag, which we placed on Bill's back, first having deprived him of his coat of mail. The laughter which was provoked by the absurd appearance of our caravan, and by the noise and contortions of the fowls, which struggled bravely for their freedom, caused us to forget the weight of our burdens on our return journey, and it was not till we had regained our dwelling that we knew how much we were fatigued.

Our thoughtful housewife soon filled a pot with potatoes, and while the children supplied the want of a cloth by covering the table with large green leaves, she milked the cow and goat, and I set the fowls at liberty, first taking care to clip their wings, lest it might occur to them to take flight.

As soon as supper was over the boys went to bed, and my wife and I were only too glad to follow their example.

CHAPTER V

SAVAGES – AND A TIGER

W HEN RETURNING from our late expedition I had observed on the beach a large quantity of timber, which it struck me we could use for the construction of a rude conveyance on which to draw our heavy stores from Tent House to the 'Nest'. The next morning, therefore, at day-break, I awoke Ernest, whom I decided to take this time as my companion; and having harnessed the donkey to a stout branch, which was intended to do duty as a sledge in the absence of a better substitute, we set out, unnoticed by the others, who still slept soundly. Arriving at the spot where the massive logs had been thrown up by the tide, we cut some into convenient lengths and placed them across the bough, which our patient donkey drew very contentedly. A small chest that we happened to notice half-buried in the sand was also added to the load. This we afterwards found to contain a quantity of sailors' clothes and some linen soaked with sea-water; but though of indifferent quality and materially injured, we gladly welcomed the addition to our wardrobe, for our supply of raiment was extremely limited.

Back at Falcon's Nest we had breakfast, and then I showed the boys how we might provide ourselves with birds, and at the same time economize our powder and shot, of which – as I took every opportunity of telling them – it required us to be very careful. My plan was to make snares from the threads which could be drawn from the agave leaves, and to place them in the branches of the trees, so as to take the birds by stratagem. This novel task had great attractions for Jack and Franz, who set to work on it immediately; while Ernest and Fritz lent me their aid in manufacturing a sledge. We had just begun our work when a loud fluttering and cackling among the poultry warned us that some unusual disturbance was going on in their neighbourhood. Suspending operations, we sought the cause of alarm, but for some time nothing was to be seen. At last Ernest, who kept his eye on Master Nip, whose movements he thought rather suspicious, noticed him apparently hiding something under one of the low bushes. On searching in the vicinity, he found a whole nest of eggs that the cunning animal had stolen as soon as they were laid; it was his last thievish raid amongst the fowls which had been the cause of the noise that we had heard. My wife could now understand how it was she had rarely been able to find an egg, and she proposed to punish the robber by tying him up every morning till the eggs were collected.

Meanwhile, Jack, who was anxious to test the utility of the snares, had mounted one of the trees and laid a few traps amid the branches. As soon as he had descended, he told us, to our great satisfaction, that the pigeons we had brought from the vessel had commenced to build near the top. On this account I forbade the boys thenceforth to fire into the tree, lest they should injure them; and I also warned them to watch lest they should get entangled in the snares.

I returned to the construction of the sledge, which, ere long, we contrived to finish. It consisted of two long beams, which were crossed by three shorter ones at equal distances from each other. At the front and back planks were nailed, so as to prevent the load from falling off; and two strong ropes were attached to the front, by which it was intended to fasten the conveyance to our beasts of burden.

I was so absorbed by my carpenter work that I failed to notice how the others were employed, and on turning round I was rather amazed to see a number of plucked ortolans hanging before the fire. Asking my wife what she intended us to do with such a quantity of birds, I was told that she was going to preserve them by roasting them and then covering them with butter, as soon as we brought home another supply. Accordingly, as soon as dinner was over, I once more selected Ernest as my companion, and, yoking the cow and ass to the sledge, we set off to our storehouse. We chose the way along the beach, and arrived without any adventure at our destination. Having unharnessed the beasts, we turned them loose, while we began to load our waggon with a powder barrel, butter cask, cheese, shot, and a set of carpenter's tools which Fritz had thoughtfully brought with him from the wreck.

Our work engrossed us so completely that we failed to notice the movements of the cow and ass, and it was only when we were ready to harness them to the conveyance that we perceived their absence. The delicate herbage on the other side of the river had proved an irresistible attraction, and they had wandered off in search of it. I despatched Ernest and Bill, which latter had insisted on accompanying us, to bring them back; and while they were away on this errand, I looked about for some small creek where we could refresh ourselves with a bath after our hot and fatiguing journey. Turning my steps towards Deliverance Bay, I succeeded in finding a place, almost surrounded by rocks, that looked most inviting. While waiting for Ernest's return, I entered a marsh which lay at the extremity of the bay, and occupied myself with cutting some fine bulrushes, with the intention of carrying them back with me to our dwelling. Looking around in search of something else which might perhaps repay me for the trouble of taking it home, I was astonished to perceive a thin curl of smoke, as of a dying fire, issuing from the swamp. Approaching the spot very cautiously, what was my alarm to see a heap of bones lying beside a few smouldering embers, round which, it was evident, human beings had sat not long before. My first thought was that perhaps God in His wise providence had guided our lost companions to this island, but this hope was banished when I noticed in the soft soil the prints of naked feet.

I had now no doubt but that the natives were again on our

track, and my heart was racked with anxiety about Ernest, of whose return there was as yet no sign. I dared not call lest my voice should attract the savages, so I could only follow silently in the direction in which he had set out, and pray to our heavenly Father to protect him. As I approached a little shrubbery that grew quite close to the bridge, I was delighted to hear a loud bark from Bill. This was succeeded by a shot, and immediately several dark forms emerged from the plantation, where they had been concealed, and on seeing me ran as fast as they could in the opposite direction, giving utterance all the while to hideous yells, and brandishing their arms wildly. As soon as they were out of sight, Ernest appeared from behind a large tree which had hidden him effectually from my view. I clasped him fondly to my heart, and asked him to tell me what had occurred since we had parted.

'As soon as I left you,' he began, 'I crossed the river, and had not gone far before I reached a beautiful grassy knoll on which the animals were quietly browsing. Feeling very hot and tired – for I had walked quickly – I lay down to rest, and soon fell fast asleep. I don't know how long I may have been sleeping, when I was awakened by a slight noise among the bushes behind us; it seemed as if a number of people were whispering softly together, and I leaned on my elbow to listen. As I raised my head I saw five savages sitting together round a small fire – before which a hedgehog was roasting – apparently engaged in earnest conversation. Sometimes

they pointed towards Tent House, sometimes in the direction of Falcon's Nest, and I knew by their gestures that we
were the subject of their discussion, and that their feelings
towards us were anything but friendly.'

'My poor boy,' I interrupted, 'how alarmed you must have
been! Did it not occur to you to repeat the fright which we
gave them before, and fire into their midst?'

'I did think of that,' he replied; 'and I was just in the act of
taking aim, when fortunately I remembered that I had only
a single charge, and that once I had lost it on them I was
helpless in their hands should they attack me. There seemed
nothing for me to do but keep still, and I hardly dared to
breathe as I lay there for what seemed to me a year, thinking
they must hear the loud beating of my heart, which almost
choked me. They were still continuing to interchange their
remarks in mysterious whispers, when a low growl made
them pause and look up. Directly in front of them stood a
large royal tiger, wagging his tail, and seeming to enjoy in
anticipation the repast which he felt sure he had within his
reach. In their terror all presence of mind forsook them, and
instead of turning the weapons – with which they were well
supplied – against the enemy, they rose and fled in wild
confusion. For a moment the animal stood as if irresolute,
then turned and followed them. Climbing a tree, I watched
the chase eagerly. For a while the savages kept the lead, but
at last the tiger, with an angry roar, increased his speed, and
gained on them rapidly. They were now on an open plain,

where there was not even a tree in whose friendly branches they might take refuge, so their lives depended on the use they could make of their limbs. The animal seemed to single out one man, and determined to make him his prey. The poor wretch, whom at this moment I could not help pitying, appeared to feel this, and redoubled his speed, now and again turning his head to see if his pursuer was still behind him. At last, evidently in despair, he faced round, and, aiming one of his poisoned arrows at the tiger, hit him in the eye. For an instant the brute stood motionless, but that instant was sufficient for his opponent. Another arrow, which took more deadly aim than the first, was hurled at him, and with a howl of agony the animal fell to the ground.

'The battle won, the victor shouted to his companions, who soon all assembled round him, and in a few minutes they directed their course towards the wood on the other side of the river. I watched their movements anxiously, and hoped soon to be able to retire from my place of concealment and return to you, as I knew you would be alarmed by my long absence. Once again, however, they looked round and paused as if startled by some strange sight, then sprang towards the shrubbery. Gazing in the same direction as they had done in order to learn the cause of their sudden disappearance, I perceived you crossing the bridge. For a moment a feeling of joy filled my heart, but the next instant I remembered that the wily red-skins were probably lying in wait for your approach, and that your life was in imminent

peril. Before you had come sufficiently near for their arrows
to reach you, I fired at random amongst the bushes, with the
result that you witnessed.'

'My brave boy!' I said. 'Your prudence has saved not only
my life, but your own, and those of the rest of our family; for
if once these savages had smelt white men's blood, they
would have taken no rest till they had made us all their
victims. I am proud of having a son on whose presence of
mind and courage I can depend in the hour of danger. Now
let us hasten home, for the day is fast drawing to a close; and
while the natives are in our neighbourhood, we must not
leave the dear ones unprotected.'

'But what about the goods which we had collected to take
back with us?' asked Ernest.

'They must remain at Tent House till tomorrow,' I replied,
'for it is now too late to admit of our returning for them.'

When we reached home and related our adventure, the
excitement of the children was extreme, and my wife was
filled with alarm at the thought that the natives might have
an attack on our dwelling in contemplation. This was really
what I dreaded myself, and in order to relieve her anxiety
and my own I decided to sit up during the night, so that their
first approach might not be unobserved. Fritz and Ernest
insisted on watching with me, and held their fire-arms in
readiness to give the invaders a warm salute; but morning
dawned without our having been disturbed.

As soon as we had partaken of breakfast, Ernest and I

again took our departure, this time resolved not to return
without our possessions. Arrived at our destination, I sent
Ernest in quest of a bag of salt, while I prepared to enjoy the
bath of which I had been deprived on the previous day. I
remained in the water for some time, but as Ernest did not
join me, as I had told him to do, I dressed hurriedly and went
to seek him, feeling pretty confident that a lazy fit had again
overtaken him, and that he had fallen asleep. I had scarcely
gone twenty yards when I heard him crying out, 'Father,
come quickly. I can't hold him any longer! He will break the
line!'

Running to his assistance, I found him lying on the sand,
hauling with both hands at a fishing line to which an enormous fish was attached, and from which it was struggling
with all its might to get free. Seizing the line, I drew the
captive into a shallow, where it was quite easy to take it. It
was a salmon, weighing at least twenty pounds; and it
pleased us to think what a welcome present this would be to
our provident housekeeper.

'How did it come that you thought of bringing your
fishing tackle with you, Ernest?' I asked, struck by his
foresight.

'I had often observed what a number of fish was to be
found hereabouts, and when leaving home this morning I
thought that if I had my line with me I might have a chance
of catching something,' he replied. 'When coming along here
I found a lot of little crabs lying on the sand, and these it

occurred to me would provide excellent bait; accordingly I
threw my line, and you arrived just in time to land the fish
which the tempting morsel had attracted.'

I praised the boy for his thoughtfulness, and then sent him
to take his turn at the bath, while I opened the salmon and
sprinkled it with salt to keep it fresh. This done, I harnessed
the animals, and as soon as Ernest reappeared we retraced
our steps homewards. We had completed about half of the
journey, and were making our way along the prairie, when all
at once our watchful companion dashed barking towards a
clump of long grass and brambles, from which a curious
animal emerged. It was nearly as large as a sheep, and moved
off by jumping rather than running. Bill pursued it as if his
honour were at stake in the race, and, getting in front of it,
made it turn and hop towards us. As it approached, Ernest
fired and killed it on the spot. We hastened to examine the
strange game that we had bagged. Its head and skin resembled those of a mouse, its ears those of a rabbit; its fore legs
were short, like the legs of a squirrel; while its hind legs
seemed disproportionately long. The length of its body was
about three feet and a half, and its tail alone measured more
than two feet. I regarded this wonderful creature closely for
some time, and could not tell to what species it belonged. At
last I noticed a pouch just below its breast, and I then felt
sure it was none other than the great kangaroo first discovered by Captain Cook in New Holland. Ernest was
anxious to preserve its skin as whole as possible, so I tied the

fore-feet together, and, passing a stick through them, bore it
to the sledge.

As soon as we came in sight of Falcon's Nest the other boys
ran out to meet us, and greeted our captive with loud cries of
astonishment. Fritz alone withheld his congratulations, and
I saw that he felt somewhat envious of Ernest, who was the
hero on this occasion.

'Father,' he said, coming up to me, 'will you take me with
you on your next expedition; while you are away we have
nothing to do, and the days seem very long. The powder is so
scarce that we must not shoot, and since yesterday morning
we only took two wild pigeons and a thrush in the traps. Do,
please, let me be your companion tomorrow?'

'I shall do so with pleasure,' I replied. 'I intend taking a
voyage to the wreck tomorrow, and I shall be glad to have
you with me.'

I then unharnessed the animals and closed them in their
stalls, hung up the kangaroo on a neighbouring tree, and,

having partaken of supper, retired with my family to our aerial dwelling.

Next morning Fritz and I prepared for our journey to the wrecked vessel.

As it was my intention to make a thorough survey of the ship this time, I told my wife that it was probable we should not return before the following day, and that therefore she must not be anxious should the evening not see us home. Then Fritz and I got into our tub, hoisted the sail, pushed from land, and, aided by the current, soon lay alongside the wreck. Our first care was to seek materials from which we could construct a more convenient raft than that which till now we had been obliged to use. Before long I had the good fortune to find a number of water barrels. We picked out a dozen of these, and fastened them securely to each other with nails and pieces of wood. On the upper side of them we laid a flooring of planks, and surrounded the whole with a handrail about a foot high; thus we had a solid raft, capable of transporting as much in a single voyage as our other boat could in three. This work occupied us almost the whole day, and by the time it was completed we were glad to retire to the cabin, where a couple of excellent mattresses invited us to repose.

Early next morning we were again afoot, and began at once our tour of inspection all over the vessel. Our own cabin was the first to be plundered. In it we found many things which, though not calculated to be very useful to us in our present circumstances, had an interest for us as souvenirs of

bygone days. In the captain's apartments we discovered a
large assortment of jewellery – watches, bracelets, necklaces,
rings – and many other articles of great value and beauty;
but these had little attraction for us as long as so many of our
everyday wants were unsupplied. Turning from this box,
from which I had taken nothing but a couple of watches,
which I intended for the children, I was pleased to find in
another many packages of different seeds, and a variety of
young European fruit trees, carefully wrapped in moss, and
evidently intended to be planted in that distant land
towards which the unfortunate vessel was directing her
course when she met her doom. Among them I recognized, to
my delight, pear, apple, and cherry trees, vine slips, and
other productions of my dear native land. These we at once
decided to take with us and try to acclimatize on our island.
A coffer full of coins scarcely attracted our attention, while
grindstones, iron bars, spades, pickaxes, and, above all, a
handmill, were carefully transferred to the boat. Locks,
bolts, window fastenings, and even the windows themselves,
were not forgotten, but were made ready for transport.
When we were preparing to start, I fortunately recollected
Ernest's last request; this was to be sure and obtain some
books from the captain's library; so, returning to the cabin, I
filled a good-sized box with volumes and placed it on board,
while Fritz increased our riches by the addition of a fishing
net, a pair of harpoons, and a line which he found by chance
on board.

CHAPTER VI

FINDING THE PINNACE

O UR RAFT was now loaded as heavily as prudence would permit, and it was not without difficulty that we got it set in motion. Happily, a favourable wind came to our aid and filled the sail that I had spread.

As we approached the island with slow and steady motion, Fritz noticed a large creature lying on the surface of the water at some distance from us, sunning itself comfortably in ignorance of our neighbourhood. Taking up my glass, I perceived that it was a turtle apparently asleep, and, at Fritz's request, I turned the course of our boat, so that we might examine it more closely. All at once, while I was engaged in arranging the sail, I felt as if the boat had received a sudden shock, and with a lurch it shot forward very rapidly.

'Why, Fritz?' I cried. 'What are you about? Do you wish to capsize us?'

Not heeding my questions, he shouted, 'I've got it! I've got it! It can't escape now, for I have harpooned it.'

'What are you talking about?' I asked. But at the same moment I observed that the harpoon, which he had thrown very adroitly, was fixed in the turtle's neck, and it was drawing us on quickly by the line. I ran forward, and, lifting my axe, meant to sever the rope and set the creature free, but Fritz begged me so earnestly not to do so, at least until it was evident our steed was about to do some damage, that I relented, and, dragged by the animal, whose agony increased its speed, we cut through the water with incredible swiftness. Perceiving at length that we were being taken out to sea, I hoisted the sail again, and, as the wind was blowing inland, the animal found the resistance too great, and directed its course towards the island. Within a gunshot of the shore we touched the bottom, and, the water being shallow, I leapt out of the boat, and cut off the turtle's head with my axe. Fritz then fired a salute with the intention of making known our arrival to those at home, and soon all ran out to greet us. Great was their astonishment to perceive not only our cargo, but the strange means by which we had brought it to land.

In order that we might remove some of our new acquisitions without delay, the two younger boys ran off for the sledge. On this primitive conveyance we placed our mattresses and the turtle, which, together, were about three hundredweight. As soon as we arrived at Falcon's Nest I set to work at once to remove the turtle from its shell. Then I cut some steaks off the flesh, and requested my wife to cook them for supper.

'I must first cut away this ugly green stuff, of which there is so much, and which looks quite disgusting,' she said.

It was with much difficulty that I could persuade her to let

the 'green stuff', which I told her was the fat of the animal, and a rare luxury, remain. She felt great repugnance, even to touching it, and assured me that if she were starving she never could taste it. Believing that, when cooked, it would be more to her mind, I told her that ere long she would consider it a most delicious dainty, and I requested her to lay the remainder of the flesh in salt, so as to preserve it for future use, and to give the head and claws to the dogs. The shell, which still remained undisposed of, had a strong attraction for the boys, and each of them longed to become its possessor.

'I am not at liberty to give it away, as it belongs by right to Fritz, who captured it,' I said. 'What do you mean to do with it, Fritz?' I asked.

'I should like to use it as a basin, which could always be kept near our house full of fresh water,' he answered.

'An excellent idea,' I said. 'But first it will be necessary to find some clay, so as to lay a solid foundation for our tank.'

'I can easily supply you with that,' interrupted Jack. 'I found a large mass of it under the root of a tree this morning. It is lying quite loosely, so that you will be spared the trouble of digging.'

'And in finding it you dirtied your face and clothes in such a manner that I was obliged to wash both you and them,' rejoined his mother, reprovingly.

'When the tank is firmly set up, I should like to lay some roots in it that I found today, and that the heat has greatly withered. I think they are a sort of radish, but I did not dare to taste them, though I saw the pig feasting on them in keen enjoyment,' said Ernest.

'That was very right,' I remarked. 'One cannot be too cautious in the use of unknown fruits and vegetables; but let me see this root.' After having examined it minutely, I said, 'If I am not greatly mistaken, you have discovered a vegetable which, even should we be deprived of every other means of subsistence, will always keep us from famine. These are the roots of the tapioca plant, from which the natives of the West Indies make a sort of bread called *cassava*. But in order to use it for this purpose, it must undergo a certain process, which removes from it a poisonous substance that it now contains. This we may be able to do in the future, and so provide ourselves with bread. But for the present let us continue to unload the sledge, so that we may bring home another portion of our freight before nightfall.'

Our second cargo consisted of two small chests, containing clothes of our own; four cart-wheels, and the handmill, which, since the discovery of the tapioca plant, we esteemed of double value.

While my wife was preparing supper for us, we set briskly to work to hoist up our mattresses to the dormitory. This was accomplished by means of the rope and pulleys without much trouble, and we found on retiring they added very materially to our comfort.

As I felt anxious concerning the safety of the raft, which was simply anchored by a couple of leaden weights, I got up before daybreak, determined to make my way to the beach while my whole family were in the enjoyment of their morning sleep. The dogs, to whom I accorded their freedom, frisked about me as if they knew I intended to start on an excursion, and were begging dumbly to be allowed to go with me. The donkey was far from displaying equal eagerness; nevertheless, I was obliged to harness him to the sledge and take him with me to the coast, where I found my possessions as I had left them. Being desirous to return to Falcon's Nest as speedily as possible, I did not load the donkey heavily, but even a light cargo seemed to be a burden to him, and he trudged lazily along, as if the previous day's work had utterly exhausted him. On arriving at the tree I was astonished to see no sign of life about our dwelling, although the sun had now advanced pretty far on his daily round. Thinking the boys must have started off in search of me, and that my wife was occupied in some household duties, I mounted the ladder. What was my amazement to see the fine hammocks still occupied, and the whole family sound asleep. I awoke them hastily, and rallied them on their heavy-headedness. 'How do you expect our work to be done if you lie till midday?' I asked, laughingly.

'You have only yourself to blame for our idleness, papa,' answered Fritz; 'for had you not provided us with such delightful mattresses, I dare say we should have been stirring hours ago.'

'Well, well! Get up now, at any rate; the sea is beautifully calm, and everything seems in favour of another trip to the wreck. Whoever is at the foot of the tree in ten minutes will be skipper on the occasion; so now every one for himself,' I said.

With a bound they all leaped on the floor, and before the appointed time Ernest, Fritz, and Jack had rejoined me below. Franz alone, therefore, was left as nominal guardian of his mother, and assumed a most important air when he heard of his trust. 'Let who dare try to do her harm as long as I am here!' he said, threateningly, as he waved an old broken pistol over his head.

'You are certainly provided with a weapon which any one would have cause to dread being turned against him,' I rejoined, laughing; 'but I am sure there will be nothing to occasion a display of your bravery before our return.'

We made a hasty breakfast, and having transported the remainder of our chattels from the beach were soon steering towards the stranded hulk. By the time we reached it, the day was so far advanced that we could only take time to secure a few articles; nevertheless, we again explored every corner of the ship, and marked those things which we wished to bring away at another time. The most important discovery that we made was that of a pinnace, carefully taken to pieces and stowed away, with all its rigging complete, and even a couple of small cannons, which might be mounted in case of necessity. This we decided to leave on board for the present, and contented ourselves with removing some household articles, such as kettles, pots, plates, glasses, and so on. To these I added a new supply of gun flints and a fresh barrel of powder. As we were about to leave the wreck, we heard Jack coming tumbling up from the hold as if heavily laden. He soon made his appearance, wheeling a barrow, which he remarked complacently would be found welcome in the potato field, and which he begged me to allow him to take home. I granted his request willingly, and sent him in search of three others, for I knew they would be found very useful when large articles were to be conveyed from one place to another. As soon as they were added to our cargo, we sailed off speedily, in order to avoid the land breeze that was rising, and which would have greatly retarded our progress.

As soon as we had landed, we loaded our barrows and
wheeled them to the Nest. Here we found an excellent supper
awaiting us, and we fell to with good appetite, while little
Franz related to us how he and his mother had passed the
time during our absence.

'What will you say, father,' he asked, 'if we soon have a
fine supply of oats and maize, pumpkins and melons?
Mamma sowed such a lot today, and she says that very soon
they will appear above the ground.'

'I should like nothing better,' I replied; 'but I think, my son, you must have been indulging in an afternoon doze, and have dreamt all this. Where in the world could your mother have got the seeds to plant?'

My wife smiled knowingly when she heard my question, and reproved the little chatterbox for having betrayed her secret.

'I meant,' she said, 'to have told you nothing of my labours, so that you might be thoroughly astonished by the discovery of the grain and vegetables; but Franz, in his ignorance, has spoiled the surprise. I found the seeds in the corner of a small box, and seeing that so much of your time was taken up in going and coming from the wreck, I thought you would not find leisure to lay out a kitchen garden for us, so I took the matter into my own hands. Franz and I chose the potato field for a site, and as we had only to pull out the roots and fill the place of each with the seed of some other plant, the job was not a very troublesome one.'

'It may not have been troublesome, but the work done is none the less useful,' I replied. 'Through your thoughtfulness we shall soon be supplied with various vegetables, which will form a very desirous addition to our daily bill of fare. But, boys, we must not allow your mother and Franz to carry away all the honour today. Get the graters which we brought from the vessel, and I shall teach you a new trade; and you, wife, would perhaps furnish us with a strong sack. If you have none ready for use, you might make one out of an old sail.'

'Certainly,' she said; 'but for what end are all these preparations?'

'I intend,' said I, 'to teach the boys the business of miller and baker, and to supply you with a batch of fresh bread. This I can do by grating down the tapioca roots, which will serve as flour. The iron plates that we brought home yesterday can be laid on the fire so as to serve as an oven.'

My wife set to work on the sack, and I spread a large sailcloth on the floor. I gave each of the boys a grater, with which I set him to rub down the roots that had been carefully washed. Soon a large mass of the vegetable lay beside us.

When a sufficient quantity of the root had been grated, I filled the sack tightly with the pollard, and sewed the ends firmly together. In order to extract the juice, which is a deadly poison, I laid the bag between two planks. I then got a long oaken beam, and having fastened one end of it to the root of a tree, drew down the opposite end as far as we could, and suspended to it the heaviest weights we possessed. This plan we found most effective, and soon the sap oozed copiously from the sack. As soon as it had ceased to run, I spread the flour in the sun to dry. Afterwards I took a small quantity of it and kneaded it into a cake, which I laid on an iron plate and hung over a brisk fire. In a short time we had a bun whose colour and odour promised a rich treat. The children begged eagerly to be allowed to taste it, but this I positively refused until we should have tried the effect of it on Nip.

'What a pity to lose such nice fresh bread on the monkey,' said Ernest. 'I am sure, father, it would not harm us in the least, it looks so good. Please give us a bit, just to see what it is like.'

'If we find that it contains nothing poisonous,' I said, 'you will get enough of it tomorrow to satisfy you.'

As soon as the cake had cooled I broke it into small pieces and threw it to the fowls and Nip; they gobbled it up with avidity, and I consequently felt sure that no quantity of it would injure us in the least. Nevertheless, I thought it prudent to wait until the morrow before partaking of it ourselves, lest the instinct of the animals should have been at fault.

The following morning we went to visit the poultry-yard, and to our great relief found our fowls as lively as ever, while the grotesque gambols of Master Nip proved that his health had undergone no alteration.

'Now, boys,' said I, 'to work immediately on our bread, and let us see how our second attempt will succeed.'

All gathered around awaiting my directions, and I distributed amongst them the utensils of which they had need. In an instant the fires were lighted, and after half an hour's active employment cakes of every size and shape were ranged on the iron trays which lay on the bright coals. The new food was pronounced delicious, and it was unanimously declared that never since we had left home had we eaten anything so excellent.

The rest of the day was employed in bringing up the remainder of our cargo from the beach, by means of the sledge and wheel-barrows, and on the following morning we set sail once more on the waters of Deliverance Bay. The idea of the pinnace continually haunted my mind, and I decided to take possession of and utilize it as speedily as possible. This was the reason why, notwithstanding my wife's scruples, I again set off to the vessel, accompanied by the three elder boys. On arriving at our destination, our primary care was to place some useful articles on the raft, so that, in case our departure should be hurried, we might not return empty-handed. The pinnace was then examined. At first I felt rather hopeless when I saw so many difficulties in the way of getting it built and launched, but these after a time disappeared one by one, and we commenced our work with great zeal. We had not advanced very far with our task when evening came upon us, and we were obliged reluctantly to return to land with our cargo. On arriving at Deliverance Bay we found my wife and Franz there to receive us.

'I have spent the whole day here,' remarked the former, 'for I wanted to be as near you as possible, and, if you see no objection to my plan, I should like to make Tent House my halting-place until your voyages to the wreck are over. While I am here I always see you on the vessel, and I shall not feel lonely as long as we can exchange signals. Besides, by our remaining on this spot the trouble of a walk will be spared you after your day's work.'

I willingly agreed to her plan, and our excursions to the wreck were made daily for at least a week. Every morning at daybreak we set out on our little craft, while my wife and Franz watched us from the shore; and every evening we returned to receive their warm welcome and congratulations on having procured such a store of riches. At length the construction of the pinnace was brought to an end, and we felt on looking at it that we were repaid tenfold for our trouble. It was elegant in shape, and looked as if it would sit lightly on the water; the rigging was complete, and at the stern was a neat half-deck. But though charming to the eye, it remained immovable on the stocks, and we knew not by what means to launch it into the sea. The sides of the vessel were so strong that the difficulty of making an opening in them seemed insurmountable, and yet for a long time this seemed to be the only thing to be attempted. At last desperation suggested an expedient which I determined to put into execution. Having found a large cast-iron mortar, such as are sometimes used by chemists, I filled it with gunpowder, and fastened a strong plank by hooks to the top of it. In this plank I cut a groove down the centre, and laid in it a slow match, made to burn for about an hour. I next caulked all the joints with tar, and thus found myself in possession of a huge petard, sufficiently powerful to open for the pinnace a way to the sea. In fear and trembling lest my plan should miscarry, and everything be destroyed, I lighted the match and then ordered the boys to get into the boat. On our arrival in the bay, just at the moment of debarkation, we heard a report like a deafening peal of thunder.

When we returned to the vessel, I observed with extreme delight that the hulk had sustained no material injury. An immense opening had been made in the side just opposite the pinnace, which was untouched, and I saw that the difficulty of launching it was completely removed.

As we had taken care when last on board to place the keel of the pinnace on rollers, it was quite easy to move it to the opening; then attaching a strong cable to its head, and fixing the other end to a solid part of the ship, we launched it into the water, where we had the satisfaction of seeing it riding gracefully on the heaving waves. All that remained to be done was to rig it with masts and sails, and this we decided to leave undone till the following day.

Two full days elapsed before the equipment of the pinnace was completed. When all was ready I gave the signal for starting, and as we approached the coast I told our amateur

sailors to announce our arrival by firing a salute. My wife, attracted by the noise, immediately appeared on the strand.

'Welcome home!' she said.

She admired our work as heartily as we could desire, and then invited us to see the results of her own occupation during the day.

Having anchored our vessel securely, we followed her a short way up the river, and were delighted and astonished at what she had accomplished. A little spot enclosed by low bushes had been laid out excellently as a kitchen garden, and the seeds planted which we had found amongst the captain's possessions.

'I chose this place,' our gardener explained, 'because the soil is light and easily dug. Here I have set potatoes and tapioca roots, on that side lettuces, and farther on I have left a bed for sugar-canes. I have also put down peas and beans, melons and cabbage seeds, and round each little plot I sowed a border of maize, so that the stems may protect the young plants from the heat of the sun.'

'Excellent!' I exclaimed. I had no idea of the surprise that was in store for us. 'The only things which your garden needs to make it perfect are the European plants that are lying at Falcon's Nest. I will bring them here as soon as possible.'

Returning to the strand, we unloaded the pinnace, and, as nothing called for a further delay at Tent House, we set out for Falcon's Nest, where we soon arrived and found everything in perfect order.

CHAPTER VII

EXCURSION TO CALABASH WOOD

A S THE evening approached the weather changed and symptoms of a storm became visible. During the night the tempest raged wildly, and even on the following morning the wind, though greatly abated, blew strongly, and the sea was considerably agitated. We therefore decided, much to my wife's delight, to spend the day on land, and I passed the morning in admiring the improvements which had been made about our dwelling during our short absence. I was greatly pleased to see that the snare had proved most efficacious, and that already had barrels of ortolans and thrushes been taken and preserved for winter use. As to the European shrubs, I found them so dry that I determined to put them in the ground at once lest we should lose them. This I did, and by the time my work was accomplished the evening was well advanced. Before retiring, we decided that the next day should be devoted to an excursion to Calabash Wood, as we wished to lay in a new stock of the useful gourd vessels. Accordingly, at daybreak our little colony was stirring, and as soon as the word of command was given our caravan set itself in motion. The donkey was harnessed to the sledge, on which we had placed the necessary provisions and ammunition for our journey. As usual, Bill led the van; behind him marched the boys, armed at all points; and my wife and I, walking on each side of the sledge, brought up the rear.

We traversed Flamingo Marsh, and reached a fertile plain beyond it. Then Fritz, who was evidently on the look-out for some exciting adventure, started off with Bill, and in a few minutes the thick undergrowth hid them both from our view. Soon, however, the loud barking of the dog told us they were at no great distance, and the next minute the report of a gun announced how Fritz was employed. A huge bird, which had been hovering in the air just above us, received the shot and fell to the ground, but, being only wounded in the wing, it got on its legs and made off again as fast as possible. Bill, seeing the prey about to escape him, dashed off after it, and having caught the fugitive, held it till his master reached the spot. The strange creature proved harder to manage than the flamingo, however, and I was called on to assist in the capture. Waiting for a favourable opportunity, I threw my handkerchief over the bird's head, and, confused by the darkness, it ceased struggling immediately. I then tied its feet and wings with a cord, and bore it in triumph to the sledge.

'Now, my young naturalist,' said I to Ernest, 'can you enlighten your brothers on the subject of our prisoner?'

'I think it is a bustard,' he replied, after examining it for a few minutes.

'And what leads you to form that opinion, which I may tell you is quite correct?' I asked.

'It has many peculiar characteristics,' was the answer,

'and amongst them are its feet, which have no spurs, but only three claws, all growing forward. The males of this species are furnished with moustaches, and from the absence of them on this one I conclude it is a female.'

'You are right,' I said. 'This is a large specimen of the female bustard. If we can cure her wounds and domesticate her, she will likely attract her mate to our dwelling, and the pair will make a desirable addition to our fowls.'

Continuing our journey, we soon arrived at Monkey Wood, where Fritz recalled, for the amusement of his mother and brothers, his adventure with the ape, and the stratagem which we had employed to procure some nuts. Meanwhile, Ernest leaned against the trunk of an old tree, and contemplated wistfully the branches overhead with their splendid load of fruit.

'What a pity the trees are so high!' he sighed, as he turned regretfully from their contemplation. 'A fly could hardly climb up that knotless trunk, and yet the fruit is so good that one is tempted to try. If I had just one nut I should be quite contented.'

He had scarcely said this when a beautiful nut fell at his feet on the grass.

'Ha! Ernest, some good fairy must have given you a wishing-cap as a birthday present, when you have only to desire and have in that fashion,' I said, smiling at his amazement.

'It looks very like it, indeed,' he replied; 'but where did it come from?'

As he was speaking a second and a third came rattling down, to the astonishment of all.

'It must be a monkey, who is trying to show his disapproval of our presence, and who is using the only weapons which he has at hand,' said Fritz, whose superior experience constituted him an authority on such subjects in the eyes of his brothers.

'No, no,' called Jack, excitedly; 'it is not a monkey. It is a horrible creature with long claws, and it is coming down the trunk. Look there!'

Jack raised the butt-end of his gun threateningly, and all regarded with curiosity the strange crab-like beast that was gliding slowly down the tree. When it was within a few feet of the ground Jack ran forward and struck at it boldly, but the blow was ill-directed, and fell upon the tree instead of on the animal. Alarmed by the assault, it scrambled down more quickly, and advanced towards its opponent with its enormous claws wide open. Then Jack suddenly pulled off his jacket, threw it on the top of the animal that was approaching him, and wrapped it tightly round. Going over to him, I helped him to despatch his enemy with the blunt end of my hatchet. The boys gathered round to examine our prize, and gave loud expression to their disgust at its appearance.

'What is the name of the hideous beast?' asked Jack.

'It is a land crab,' I replied. 'A sort of animal for which you seem to have a particular fancy, for this is the second affray you have had with one of the species. Animals of this kind are often to be found on cocoa-nut trees, the fruit of which they use for food. They break off the nuts, as you have seen this one do, and throw them on the ground, expecting the fall to break the shell, as it often does.'

We then placed a few of the nuts, together with the crab, on the sledge, and, after having refreshed ourselves with a little cocoa-nut milk, proceeded on our journey. Our progress was very slow, for our path became every yard more intricate, and often we were obliged to use our axes, and cut a road for the donkey and his conveyance. At length we arrived at Calabash Wood. We halted on the same spot that Fritz and I had formerly found so pleasant. My wife and children were greatly astonished at the immense growth of the trees and their remarkable fruit. Having gathered a large number of gourds, we began our vessel manufacture at once. After having showed my sons how to make plates and basins, which I considered to be the most easily formed articles, I occupied myself with constructing an egg-basket and a cheese-tray, both of which turned out very successfully. Dishes, spoons, and milk-vessels were not forgotten.

While we were busy in manufacturing these various articles, Fritz and Jack begged me to allow them to cook the crab for dinner. This they assured me they could do by adopting the plan of the savages, of which I had told them – that is, to heat the water with red-hot stones. I gave them leave to try their skill, but while they were preparing the gourd in which they intended to boil it, they remembered that they had no water, and asked me if I knew of any little spring close at hand where they could procure some. I set out along with them in search of one which I had found on my last visit, and which I thought could not be far away. Jack went on ahead, and suddenly let out a cry: 'Papa, papa! A crocodile!'

'My dear child, what an absurdity!' I said, laughing. 'Fancy a crocodile in a place where we cannot find even the smallest stream! What are you thinking about?'

'It does seem queer,' he replied, looking quite scared; 'but if this is not a crocodile, I'll never be sure of anything again. It is lying asleep on a rock. Just come with me and see for yourself.'

I followed the boy, who was evidently greatly frightened, and found that what he had supposed to be a crocodile was in reality an immense lizard, known as the iguana. It is common in the West Indies, and is looked on there as a great dainty. Fritz raised his gun with the intention of firing on the spot, but I prevented him.

'The iguana is very tenacious of life,' I said, 'and it is possible the shot would not take any effect on it. I shall try and put into execution a plan that is generally adopted in the countries in which this animal is often found, and by which I think we can make sure of our quarry.'

Thereupon I cut a strong rod, and attached a piece of string to the end of it. This I twisted into a running noose. The animal still slept, and I approached it softly, whistling. The lizard awoke, but lay motionless as if fascinated by the music, which I am sure a less lenient critic would have considered very unmelodious. Seeing my advantage, I advanced quickly, and, slipping the noose round the animal's neck, drew the cord tightly. The iguana struggled for some time, but with the help of the boys I soon overcame it, and made myself master of the new species of game. The curious creature was more than five feet in length, and proved a very unwieldy burden. I was obliged to carry it on my back, for want of any other means of locomotion, and Fritz and Jack, with the desire of lightening my load, held up its tail.

My wife had by this time become alarmed by our lengthened absence, and as we neared the spot where we had left her, we heard her and Franz shouting on us loudly, as if thus they would keep themselves from feeling lonely. She was delighted at our return, and listened gladly to a recital of our adventures.

'But where is the water,' she asked, 'in search of which you set out?'

We laughed heartily at our stupidity when her question recalled our forgotten errand to our minds, and we suggested that, as a punishment, we should have nothing to eat; but this she would not agree to.

'You must be hungry by this time,' she said, 'and you will be contented, I hope, with a cold meal, since we cannot manage to provide a warm one.'

After we had partaken of the provisions set before us by

my wife, we prepared to return home. The day was so far advanced that we decided to leave the sledge, which we knew would materially retard our progress, in the wood till the following day, and contented ourselves with loading the donkey with Franz – who was by this time very tired – a few of the vessels that we had made, the iguana, and the bustard. These arrangements effected, we commenced our return journey. By the time the sun had gone down we had arrived at Falcon's Nest, and after partaking of part of the iguana – the flesh of which we found excellent – we retired to our hammocks among the branches.

CHAPTER VIII

MAKING CANDLES

O N THE following morning I set out along with Fritz, to bring home the sledge with the remainder of the gourd vessels. At Calabash Wood we found all the vessels that we had left undisturbed and ready for use. As it was still early in the day, we decided to make an excursion to that part of the island which we had not yet explored. Owing to the thick growth of underwood, through which it was almost imposs-ible for us to make our way, we advanced but slowly. Many curious sights attracted our attention as we passed. Tapioca and potatoes grew on every side; whole tribes of agoutis sported round the trunks of the trees; flowers of every form and hue looked up at us temptingly; but none of these things could we stop to regard if we wished to attain our object before nightfall. At the entrance to a pretty little grove a small bush, covered thickly with white berries, struck Fritz as so uncommon and unlike anything he had seen before, that he begged me to halt for a moment and examine it. The berries were covered with a waxy substance, that stuck to our fingers when we touched it. From botanists' descriptions of the shrub I knew it to be the *Myrica Cerifera*, or wax-bearer.

'Why, Fritz, this is a treasure,' I said joyfully. 'From these berries it is possible to make candles that will burn as well as those made out of bees' wax. How delighted your mother will be with this discovery!'

When Fritz heard this he collected an ample supply of the fruit of the wax-tree, and placed it in a bag on the donkey's back.

Arriving at another small wood, we saw some trees that were entirely unknown to us. They looked like wild fig trees, and grew to a prodigious height, while from their bark oozed a resinous substance, that seemed to have become hardened by the air, and stuck to the trunk in little balls.

Fritz broke off one of these and rubbed it between his fingers. What was his surprise to find that the heat rendered it quite soft, so that he could stretch it without breaking it.

'I do believe this is an india-rubber tree, father,' he said. 'Look at what I have here; it is quite elastic.'

I examined the substance myself, and found that he was not mistaken. 'You are right,' I replied; 'and your discovery is very important. This is a specimen of the caoutchouc tree, from which the india-rubber flows.'

'But, father, why do you say it is important to us to find it? I don't think bits of india-rubber can do us much good.'

'Don't form conclusions too hastily, my boy. This liquid can be made into bottles and vessels of various kinds. I might even turn shoemaker, and provide you with a pair of caout-chouc shoes.'

We placed a few calabash basins round the tree, expecting them to be filled on our return, and continued our journey.

For some time we marched on without adventure or discovery, but towards midday we arrived at a cocoa palm grove. Amongst the trees I observed some whose leaves were covered with a white dust resembling flour. In the trunk of one of them that the wind had blown down I saw a quantity of whitish-coloured powder, which I immediately guessed to be sago. To confirm me in this opinion I discovered amid the powder some of those small fat worms which make their home in the sago tree, and which the Indians consider a great delicacy. I determined to test their taste in the matter, and spitted a few of the grubs on a thin stick which I hung over the fire that Fritz had just kindled. Before long the roast sent forth such a savoury odour that the dish, instead of disgusting us, as Fritz prophesied it would be sure to do, tempted us very much; and we found that a repast of sago worms and potatoes was by no means to be despised by a hungry man.

We gathered a large quantity of the sago, as we knew it would be welcome to our housekeeper, and then returned to the gourd wood. There we harnessed the donkey to the sledge, placed all our treasures on it – amongst them were the vessels filled with caoutchouc, which had already become quite solid – and without further adventure arrived at Falcon's Nest, where we and our possessions received a warm greeting. My wife was greatly pleased when I told her that soon I could provide her with a substitute for candles.

'You could give me nothing that I should like better,' she

said as she regarded the bag with approval. 'Pray begin your chandler's business at once, as, now that you have put the idea into my head, I shall have neither rest nor peace till I have obtained the promised lights.'

I agreed to set about the manufacture of them on the morrow, and we all looked forward gladly to the time when we should not be obliged to go to bed at sunset, as we now were.

Morning had scarcely dawned when the children, who

always looked forward impatiently to every new employment that was in prospect, awoke me, and reminded me of
last night's promise. As soon, therefore, as I was dressed I
called them all together, and allotted to each his part in the
work. In the first place, I filled a large cauldron with water
and berries, and hung it over the fire. In a short time the
waxy substance melted and rose to the surface. This I
skimmed off carefully and placed near the fire to keep it from
congealing, until my wife should have ready the wicks which
she was making from threads of sailcloth. We twisted a
number of these threads together, and then dipped them
several times into the wax. Afterwards they were hung in the
air to dry. As soon as the first coating was hard the dipping
process was repeated continuously until there was a sufficient thickness of wax round the wicks. In this way we
provided ourselves with a good number of lights, which,
though not by any means perfect in form, freed us nevertheless from the undesirable necessity of relinquishing our work
at sundown, and enabled us to add many useful hours to our
day.

My success as a chandler encouraged me so much that I
determined to try and put another project which I had
formed into execution. For some time my wife had been
troubled to see the cream put to no good use and she had
often asked me if I could not possibly invent something
which might be made to serve in place of a churn. It now
struck me that we might imitate successfully the plan of the

Hottentots, who put their cream in a skin and shake it till the butter is produced. As we had no skin that we could employ for that purpose, I selected a large gourd, filled it with the cream, corked it hermetically, and then gave it to the boys to shake. They turned their work into play by placing the gourd in the middle of a square piece of sailcloth, and each taking a corner, they rocked it slowly backwards and forwards, until I thought the improvised churn must have done its work. On uncorking the gourd my wife was delighted to find that we had a pound or two of excellent butter, and the boys, who now saw a probability of always having a supply of the favourite substance on hands, were no less pleased.

Another want, which we had always thought and talked of supplying, was that of a small cart to take the place of the sledge, that was quite unfitted for some roads, and that the animals had great difficulty in drawing. As we had brought wheels with us from the wreck, the job was not so difficult as it might otherwise have been. In a day or two I completed a two-wheeled car, which, though clumsy and ugly, was a marked improvement on our first vehicle.

While I was occupied in this way my wife and children were busy transplanting the fruit trees which I had stuck down at random, merely with the intention of keeping the roots moist. The vines were set round the roots of our trees, as we expected their foliage would ward off from the tender plants the burning rays of the sun. Of the chestnuts, walnuts, and cherries we formed an avenue leading from Falcon's

Nest to the bridge, and round Tent House we planted a
number of native shrubs, as we thought they were strong
enough to bear heat and drought. Thus we transformed a
barren shore into a delightful shady retreat. We also surrounded the tent with a thick hedge of prickly plants, to
prevent it being attacked, at any rate by wild beasts.

This work of cultivation and improvement occupied us for
six weeks. But while we changed the appearance of our island
very much for the better, we changed that of our clothing
very materially for the worse. Consequently, as soon as our
farming operations were at an end, it was time to think of
another voyage to the wreck in search of necessary covering
for our half-naked bodies. Accordingly, on the first calm day,
we embarked in our pinnace, which shot through the water
with astonishing ease and lightness. On examining the wreck
we found that time was laying its hand upon it, and that a
recent storm had seriously damaged many chests of clothes
and powder. It was quite evident the old hulk could not hold
out much longer, so we decided to take away everything that
was likely to be useful to us, and then to blow up the vessel,
so that the timber might float to the shore. It required us to
make many voyages before we had got possession of everything; but at the end of three days almost all that the vessel
contained had been transported to land. When this was done
I placed a barrel of gunpowder in the hold, and attaching to
it a slow match, lighted at one end, I returned hastily to the
pinnace and made for the shore. Darkness had not long

succeeded day when a terrible explosion, followed by the appearance of a column of fire that shot up from the sea to the clouds, announced the destruction of the gallant ship.

It seemed then as if the last link that bound us to the Fatherland was broken, and we could not help shedding bitter tears as we thought of our isolated position, and the wide stretch of ocean that separated us from all we used to hold so dear. We retired to rest feeling very sad, and longing more earnestly than we had yet done for some means of returning to our beautiful mountain valley in Switzerland.

CHAPTER IX

BUFFALOES AND A JACKAL

O N THE following day my expectations were verified, and the shore was strewed with fragments of the wreck. Several copper boilers, which we had been unable to bring away in the pinnace, and which I had attached to large empty casks, in the hope that the current would drive them in our direction, had also been cast upon the beach, much to my satisfaction.

For several days we were occupied in collecting these waifs and strays. While my wife was lending us her aid one afternoon, she discovered that two of her geese and one duck, which had lately scarcely been seen, had each hatched a brood of young close to the strand. It was not without considerable difficulty that she made herself mistress of the fowls, and carried them to Falcon's Nest, whither we were all glad to return. On the way I noticed that the fruit trees that we had lately planted between our dwelling and the bridge required props, as their stems were very slender, and I decided to set out next morning in search of some bamboos with which to support them.

No sooner did I mention my intention than it was clear I must take the whole family with me, one and all having an especially good reason why he or she should make one of the party. Our supply of candles was nearly exhausted. We therefore required some more wax berries, for my wife now devoted her evenings to needlework, and I always wrote my journal by candlelight.

On the following morning therefore we all set off together. We used the cart which I had made for the first time; and a couple of planks put across it made a very comfortable seat for the weak or tired ones of the party. The cow and the ass passively submitted to be harnessed to it, and pulled together excellently. In order to render ourselves independent of monkeys and crabs for the delicious fruit of the cocoa palm, and to enable the boys to climb the smooth trunks, I had made some coverings for their legs and arms from the rough skin of the shark, and these also I took with me.

We threaded our way through the potato plantation and guava wood, and made our first halt at the spot where the much-prized wax-tree grew abundantly, and we gathered our harvest of berries in no time. Two bags were filled with them, and these we hid in a hollow tree, intending to take them up on our return. Then we proceeded through the caoutchouc grove to an open plain.

As soon as we had unharnessed the wearied beasts of burden, and set them free to graze on the rich herbage that grew beneath the palms, we set out towards the marsh, where we wished to cut some bamboos. We stripped them of their leaves, and having tied them up in bundles placed them on the cart. This hard work gave the boys an appetite, but as their mother had not yet prepared any food for us, they were obliged to trust to their own exertions for finding wherewith to satisfy their hunger.

'I don't see a thing that even a savage could eat,' said Jack, looking about him in all directions. 'Of course there are plenty of cocoa-nuts, but they might as well not be there, since we can't reach them, for we may not expect to fall in with an obliging crab every day, who will drop them at our feet.'

'Certainly not,' I remarked; 'but had you not better attempt the ascent yourself? I think I could put you on a plan of reaching the top, if you are very anxious to do so.'

The boys all testified their eagerness to mount the tree, so I bound pieces of the shark's skin on their legs and arms, and showed them how to knot a cord round the trunk as they ascended, in order to rest when they grew tired of climbing. By these means they soon reached the summit, and with their axes sent down a perfect shower of nuts, upon which we regaled ourselves; so the store of provisions that we had brought with us remained untouched.

The day being advanced, we decided to pass the night on this charming spot, and set about erecting a hut of boughs as a slight protection from the cold and dew. While we were thus occupied, the ass, who had been quietly grazing close at hand, burst out into a loud 'he-haw', and, tossing his head and kicking his heels in the air, set off at a mad gallop. We ran after him for a short distance, but as it was getting dark, and no trace of him was to be seen, we were obliged to return to the tent, greatly disturbed by his disappearance. The loss of the animal which had been of such infinite service to us since we had landed on the island, as well as the fear which his sudden flight had aroused lest some dangerous beast should be in our vicinity, troubled us deeply. To guard against the approach of possible foes, I kindled a large fire in front of our camp and watched till daybreak. But the night passed without any disturbance.

After breakfast I whistled on the dogs, and, having selected Jack to be my companion, started in search of 'Grizzly', as Franz had christened the ass. After looking vainly for half an hour, I discovered the prints of the fugitive's shoes; but these, after a little, became mixed with other tracks, and I knew he had fallen in with a troop of animals of some sort. Following the marks, we reached a wide plain, and in the far distance we could distinguish, by the aid of the telescope, a herd of what seemed to me not unlike horses. Thinking it probable that this might be the very company to which our truant friend had joined himself, I resolved to go nearer. When we were within about a hundred paces of the animals I recognized them to be buffaloes.

Knowing the natural ferocity of these beasts, I felt greatly alarmed, and decided that it was best to use discretion, and retire from the field. This, however, I saw I should have some difficulty in doing, for the animals stood directly opposite us, and moved as we did, regarding us all the time rather in surprise than in anger.

For a short time we contemplated each other, neither party seeming to know how to act. All at once the dogs, which, until now, had stayed in our rear, darted past us barking furiously. The noise seemed to arouse the whole herd. They rushed hither and thither, uttering frightful bellowings, and pawed the ground impatiently with their hind feet, scattering little tufts of grass and lumps of clay in the air. The dogs appeared in no way daunted by this angry display, but, rushing amongst the band, seized a young buffalo calf and dragged it to the ground. Its dam, thoroughly enraged, came to its help, and was about to take revenge on its assailants, when I levelled my gun and fired. The effect was electric. The whole herd stood still for a moment, then, wheeling round, dashed at a headlong pace through the river, and did not pause as long as they were in sight. In a few minutes the only indications of their existence were the echoes of their distant roars.

Now that the probability of being injured by them was removed, I turned my attention to the mighty animal which I had wounded, and which lay rolling on the sand, and I put an end to her life by discharging my pistol between her eyes. The dogs still retained their hold on their prize, but I saw that the lengthened struggle they had had with it had exhausted their strength, and I was about to administer the

same treatment to it that I had to its dam, when Jack prevented me, saying, 'Oh, please don't kill it! It is so young that I think we might tame it, if you would only let us. Do let me take it home, father!'

Thinking that it might be possible to improve on its savage condition, and turn it into quite a useful carrier, I laid down my pistol, and, waiting for a favourable opportunity, threw my lasso, so as to twist the cord round the calf's legs. Then I gave it a sudden jerk. The animal fell to the ground, and I replaced the lasso with a stronger cord; I also bound the forelegs loosely.

Jack thought our chief difficulty was over when we had got this accomplished, but I knew that to make our prisoner follow us would be no easy task. Thinking how I could manage this, a plan occurred to me that I had often heard of being adopted in Italy to tame wild bulls, and which, though cruel, was the only sure one that I knew. I therefore resolved to try it. Aided by Jack, I pierced a hole in the buffalo's nostrils with the point of my knife, and through it I passed a strong cord, which I tied to a tree. The pain of the operation caused the animal to struggle violently for a little, but soon it became quite quiet, and I found that I could lead it unresistingly wherever I wished.

As we were about to leave the place, Jack attracted my attention to the carcass of the dead beast, which I had quite forgotten, by asking me if it was not possible to use its flesh for food. Unfortunately it was impossible for us to take the whole animal with us, as we had no means of carrying it; so I cut away the tongue and some pieces of the flesh, and left the remainder for the hungry dogs to feast on. They were not allowed undisputed enjoyment of it, however, for ere many minutes the air seemed black with vultures and other birds of prey, which settled down like a cloud on the carcass, and between whom and the dogs a spasmodic contest was carried on. For a moment hostilities would be suspended, while all dined with good appetite, but the next instant a bark from pugilistic Bill was the signal for the interruption of the meal and renewal of the skirmish.

As soon as Topsy and Bill had satisfied their appetites, and we had cut a number of bamboos with which I intended to fashion some candle moulds, we set off on our return. As we were climbing a little hill a short distance farther on, Jack, who seemed to have the eye of a lynx whenever anything that gave him an excuse for firing a shot turned up, said, 'Surely that is a jackal! It seems just like those that surrounded our tent the first night we spent on the island. What do you think?'

'I believe you are right,' I replied, as I saw a large animal winding its way through a narrow pass in the rocks. 'It is probably a female making for her den, and if we exercise caution we might follow her to the place without attracting her notice.'

This was not to be, however, for ere she had advanced far the dogs were upon her, and before I could get them called off she had fallen a victim to their strength and courage. A low cry in the bushes on our right led us to the nest, and in it lay several little cubs, who blinked at us sleepily with their half-open eyes. Jack begged earnestly to be permitted to take one home to rear, and I consented willingly, as I reflected that, if properly trained, it might be of great assistance to us on our hunting expeditions.

It was late in the afternoon when we rejoined our family, and endless were the questions asked and answered concerning our adventures. The buffalo and jackal caused much excitement among our little band, and Jack was regarded as a conquering hero.

As it was now too late for us to think of returning to Falcon's Nest, we were obliged to make preparations for passing a second night on this unprotected spot. Fortunately the boys had collected a heap of wood during the day, so as far as a blazing fire could render us safe we should have nothing to fear.

While we were seated at supper I asked my wife how she and the children had spent the time during my absence, and it was with extreme pleasure that I heard of their industry. Fritz had gone to explore the rocks about Cape Disappointment, and had taken a splendid bird, which Ernest pronounced to be a Malabar eagle. Ernest had cut and tied a great quantity of bamboos, and had, besides, hewn an enormous tree which he thought was a sago palm. My wife herself had gathered a lot of cocoa-nuts and acorns, which she

wished to take home. However, the day had not passed
wholly without accident, for while they were out of the hut
engaged on their different occupations a band of monkeys
entered it, and did as much injury as they could. A gourd full
of wine that my wife was keeping for my refreshment was
overturned; the fruit which we had collected was scattered
here and there, and a great portion of it stolen; and the hut
itself had received so much damage that it took them more
than three hours to repair it.

As soon as we had finished supper we kindled our watch-
fire in front of our temporary dwelling, and hung a piece of
buffalo flesh in the smoke, so that it might be perfectly cured.
The young calf received a dish of milk and potatoes, and
seemed to appreciate the novel food greatly; he then lay
down peacefully beside the cow, while the dogs stretched
themselves before the fire, ready to sound the alarm in case of
necessity. We then retired to our mossy beds, and soon were
in the enjoyment of profound sleep. On the following morning I was about to give the order for marching when my wife
reminded me of the sago palm that Ernest had felled, and
asked me if we had not better secure its contents.

'If this trunk really contains the valuable pith from which
sago is made, is it not a pity to leave it here untouched?' she
asked. 'Its contents are so delicious and strengthening that I
shall quit the place regretfully unless we have a portion of
them with us.'

I hesitated a little before speaking. To split open the

enormous trunk would be a wearisome job, and would, I knew, occupy us the whole day, so that a third night must be spent away from the Nest; but, on the other hand, as my wife said, it would be a pity not to possess ourselves of the sago. After short deliberation I decided to remain, so summoning the boys, and collecting such tools as we required, we set off to the place where the tree lay. It required Herculean efforts to cleave it open; but at last the task was accomplished. Then we made one of the ends of the tree into a trough, and in this we placed the pith as we extracted it. Afterwards we moistened it with water, and kneaded it like dough. When the paste appeared to be of the proper consistency, I attached one of our large graters at the end of the trough, and squeezed the wet mixture through it. It oozed out at every hole like hailstones; these we caught in a cloth, and laid in the sun to dry. While engaged on this manufacture, it occurred to me that the two halves of the trunk might be made into gutters, with which we could bring water from Jackal River for watering our garden at Tent House. I resolved at least to take them with me and try the experiment. As soon as darkness had again fallen around us we lighted our fires and retired for the night.

Next morning, Jack, Fritz, Ernest, and I set out early to our fruit-tree plantation, and took with us a load of bamboos with which to prop the drooping plants; my wife remained at home with little Franz, and promised to have a good dinner of sago for us on our return.

When we arrived at that part of the avenue where the weakest trees grew we found that our care was very much needed, for the fierce winds which for some days past had been blowing from the sea had bent the slight stems almost to the ground. We raised them gently, and propped them up firmly with bamboos, which we drove into holes made in the earth with a crowbar.

Towards noon we finished our labours, and then returned to the Nest. We found our housekeeper's promise fulfilled, and a pleasant repast of buffalo's flesh and boiled sago awaiting us. As we were enjoying our well-earned dinner I heard a noise outside, and sent Jack to the door to ascertain the cause of it. At first he could see nothing, but in a minute he rushed back into the tent, shouting, 'The savages! The savages!' and seeming to be half out of his mind with terror. Thinking that we had given good cause to the red-skins to know that we could not be attacked with impunity, I was greatly amazed at their return, and went to the entrance myself in order to see whether Jack had been deceived or not. Though nothing was visible, the yells and shrieks that reached my ear led me to conclude that our persevering foes were without doubt in our neighbourhood, and that a quarrel had arisen amongst themselves. Seizing my gun, I descended the staircase, followed by Fritz and Ernest, and approached the spot from whence the sounds issued. On arriving at a little turn in the path, fancy our surprise on discovering – not a band of savages engaged in mortal combat, as we had supposed, but a troop of orang-outangs, who were avenging themselves on a few young elephants for having invaded their territory and disturbed them at their repast, and who sat chattering and grinning on the branches of the oak trees, as they pelted the huge offenders with sticks, acorns, or anything that came within their reach. The elephants seemed thoroughly amazed by this unexpected attack, and stood looking around stupidly, as if not knowing what means of defence to adopt; then, turning towards the open plain, they moved their colossal bodies slowly out of sight, and the apes were left in undisturbed possession of their abode.

Greatly relieved and amused by this sight, we returned to the Nest, and passed the evening in completing some little arrangements outside our dwelling, as well as in increasing our stock of candles, which was disappearing rapidly. Then we retired for the night.

CHAPTER X

GRIZZLY AGAIN

A S WE were seated at breakfast my wife recalled a conversation that we had had some days previously, when we had partly resolved to construct a new and safer staircase by which to reach our tent.

'I am always in fear of some accident happening,' she said. 'The boys never seem to heed my warnings, but run up and down like wild cats, as if it were not possible for them to miss a step and get severely hurt. It would relieve my mind very much if you could invent some other plan of ascending to our dwelling.'

'The same thought has been troubling me not a little lately,' I answered, 'but I cannot hit on any practicable way of improving our ladder. As it now is, it has one great advantage, which is, that we can pull it up after us, and so render our Nest an unconquerable fortress; whereas, if we constructed a solid flight of steps, it would, of course, be impossible to remove them at will, and an easy and inviting entrance would thus be made to our very door.'

'That is, to be sure, a serious drawback; but if the plan of which I have been thinking be feasible, it may be overcome,' said my wife. 'The other day I heard you telling the children that there is a swarm of bees inside the trunk. Now, if this be the case, it must necessarily be hollow. Would it not be possible, then, to form a staircase inside, which would be both safe for the children and hidden from the natives?'

'Your idea is most ingenious, if it could only be carried out,' was my reply. 'I shall go and sound the trunk, and ascertain how large the cavity really is.'

The boys followed me, and, climbing like young squirrels to the tops of the roots, began tapping on the bark, in order to judge from the sound of the size of the hole. Alas, their zeal met with a poor reward! The noise which they made proved anything but agreeable to the bees inside. A countless army swarmed out and made a furious attack on their disturbers; buzzed venomously around them; alighted on their faces, hands and hair in scores, and stung them most severely. Poor Jack, as usual, came off worst in the fray. In a few minutes his face was quite inflamed, but he bore the pain manfully, while Ernest howled loudly over the few stings he had received. My wife calmed the uproar, and covered their wounds with fresh, damp earth; this gave them wonderful relief, but it was several hours before the acute pain subsided.

When the boys became a little better, their desire to have revenge on the insects that had treated them so badly grew very strong, and they begged me to hasten my preparations for getting possession of the honey. While the bees still hummed angrily around the tree, I got ready some tobacco, a pipe, chisel, hammer, clay, and several other things which

were necessary for the carrying out of my plan. Out of a large
gourd I formed a hive, which I placed on a stand and covered
with a straw roof. I filled up with clay all the openings in the
trunk, except a very small one, and in it I inserted the bowl of
my pipe, and puffed the tobacco smoke into the nest so as to
stupefy its occupants. At first there was a loud buzzing like
the sound of a distant drum, but little by little it subsided,
and profound stillness, which told me the tobacco had done
its work, succeeded. We then proceeded to cut away a piece
of the trunk, but before removing it I repeated the fumiga-
tion lest the insects should revive during our operations.
When I considered they had been sufficiently lulled, I separated from the tree the piece that I had cut out, thus exposing
to view the wonderful work of the bee colony. The quantity
of wax and honey that they had collected was so great that
we hardly knew how to dispose of it. The honeycombs, with
which the interior of the tree was lined, I cut off carefully and
placed in a cask that I had previously thoroughly cleansed
for the purpose. The upper combs, in which the bees had
clustered, I put into the gourd, which I intended should
serve as a hive, and placed it on a plank that Ernest had
raised for it. Thinking that as soon as the insects recovered
from their stupefaction they would instinctively return to
their old abode, and wishing to prevent this, I placed some
burning tobacco in the hollow of the tree. This I imagined
would prevent their near approach. As I expected, in a short
time they issued from the gourd in a body and flew towards
the tree, but the fumes of the hated plant drove them away,

and after a while they settled down quietly in their new home, and began to work on their own account and on ours. This new possession, which promised by multiplying itself to provide us with a supply of honey and wax for the future, afforded us great satisfaction.

The next morning we set to work without further obstruction on the formation of the stairs. On probing the trunk I was pleased to find that it was hollow from the roots to the branches, and that it was wide enough to admit of a winding staircase being built inside. Aided by the boys, I commenced operations that very day. Our first care was to cut an opening in the bark, just the size of one of the doors that we had brought from the wreck. This we did on the side facing the sea. We then cleared the cavity of all the decayed wood that had lodged in it for so long, and fixed in the centre a stout beam which reached to the branches, and round which we intended to carry the stairs. With mallet and chisel we made deep notches both in the trunk and the central beam, and in these we nailed the steps that we had made beforehand from the staves of a barrel. In order to admit light into the tower, I cut a few holes in the tree, and in these I fixed the windows that we had found in the vessel. The construction of this flight of steps occupied us unremittingly for a couple of weeks, but when it was completed it gratified us to think that our time and labour had not been spent in vain; for, though by no means elegant in design, the stairs were solid and convenient, and that was all we desired.

In the meantime an addition had been made to our domes-

tic animals, in the shape of a couple of fine puppies of pure
Danish breed that Topsy had presented to us. I allowed Jack
to put his jackal to feed with them, and to this Topsy made
no objection. She gave the little stranger a friendly welcome
to her nest, and treated her adopted child with maternal
affection and care.

A few days after this event our flocks were enlarged by two
kids and five lambs, so we had no cause to fear the extermina-
tion of our livestock.

In order to prevent the loss of any of our prized animals,
should it occur to them to follow the example of the errant
donkey, I got the boys to fasten round the neck of each a
couple of little bells that we had found when last on board the
vessel, and that we had brought with us, intending them for
trading with the natives. These, I thought, would soon put
us on the track of the fugitives.

A great part of my leisure time was taken up now with the
young buffalo, which I was anxious to train to be a useful
beast of burden. The incision that I had made in his nose was
quickly healed, so I passed through the hole, after the
manner of the Hottentots, a small rod, which served as a bit,
and to the end of it I fastened ropes. By this means I could
lead him whither I would, though often he proved anything
but a docile follower. To habituate him to the loads which in
the future he would have to bear, I covered his back with a
sailcloth, which I fastened firmly round him with a strap,
and in it I packed a number of heavy articles, with which he

marched on quite contentedly. As the children were desirous
of converting him at times into a saddle-horse, I accustomed
him at first with Nip for a rider. It was well that I did so, for
this new burden met with but little approval from him. He
balanced himself on his fore feet, while he raised his hind feet
in the air, and tried every means of freeing himself of the
unwelcome load. But Nip held his place fearlessly, and
showed his enjoyment of his steed's vain efforts to get rid of
him by making all sorts of absurd grimaces. By degrees,
however, the animal grew accustomed to his rider, and in a
few days had become so tractable and quiet that the boys
bestrode him without fear.

As the winter was now approaching, I devoted a part of
my leisure time to the manufacture of candles, which I made
this time partly of bees' wax and partly of that obtained
from the berries. We had some difficulty in providing ourselves with wicks, as our prudent housewife refused to permit us to use any of the small remaining piece of sailcloth for
that purpose. After various experiments, it struck me that
we might utilize a very inflammable kind of wood, called in
the Antilles 'firewood'. I cut some thin sticks of this, and
placed them in the moulds; but my wife, who did not look
favourably on these wooden wicks, suggested that I should
try instead some threads pulled out of the leaves of the
karata plant that she had dried in the sun. Having laid these
different sorts of wicks in the reed moulds, we poured the
liquid wax over them, and left them in the air to harden.

As soon as night came I lighted a candle of each sort, in order to see how they would burn. Unfortunately, neither of them was as good as the old ones, for the firewood burned away too quickly, while the karata flickered and threatened every moment to go out entirely. However, we were obliged to content ourselves with them until chance should point out to us some means of obtaining cotton otherwise than by using the very limited piece that we had.

After this experiment I was tempted to try my ingenuity in making a pair of shoes, and I encouraged the boys to make some caoutchouc bottles in the same way. First, I obtained an old pair of stockings, and having packed them tightly with sand, I covered them with a thin coating of clay, and placed them in the sun to dry. I then fastened on a pair of stout buffalo leather soles, and with a brush made of goat's hair laid on layer after layer of the india-rubber gum until it had attained the necessary thickness. Afterwards I hung them up in the air, and when the caoutchouc had solidified I shook the sand out of the stockings, broke off the hardened clay, and found myself the possessor of a pair of soft, warm, and water-tight boots. The children shouted with joy when they saw them completed and one and all begged me to supply them each with a similar pair. This I promised to do as soon as we could obtain a further supply of the necessary india-rubber liquid.

The drawing of the water from the river for domestic purposes was often the cause of much grumbling among the

children, so, as I wished to remove the cause of dispute, I
connected the stream with the fountain by means of the
palm-tree ducts that we had brought from the wood for the
purpose. In the upper part of the river we raised a sort of
dam, whence the water flowed into our canal, and was
received in the tortoise-shell vessel that stood quite close to
the door. To prevent an overflow we fastened to the basin a
cane pipe, through which the redundant water passed.

One morning, just as we had assembled after breakfast,
and were about to arrange our plans for the day, our attention was arrested by most unusual sounds, which proceeded
from the neighbouring wood, and which seemed like a ming-
ling of howls and hisses, ending in a lamentable wail. Fearing an attack from some terrible beast of prey, we each seized
our guns, in order that we might be prepared to defend
ourselves. Fritz, Ernest, and I took our stand at the foot of
the tree, while the others sought the shelter of our castle
amid the branches. For several minutes perfect silence
reigned; then the discordant noises were repeated, this time
nearer and louder. It seemed as if only a few low shrubs
separated us from the noisy disturber of our peace. Topsy
and Bill crouched whining under the roots of the tree, and
the children awaited the moment of action tremblingly.
Suddenly from amongst the long grass bounded the dreaded
monster, and Ernest set up a howl of terror, but Fritz threw
down his gun and, clapping his hands in delight, called,
'Mother, mother, you may come down from your perch. It is

neither a lion nor a bear, but only poor old Grizzly, who has grown tired of his freedom, and longs again for his panniers.'

However, I was not fully assured that the noises which we had heard had been produced by our donkey alone, and I stood listening so as to hear if the sounds should be repeated. In a minute the same howl and wail were audible as before, and from the neighbouring wood issued a fine onagra, or wild ass. Without delay I decided to capture the beautiful animal and try to tame it. When it first noticed us it appeared to be greatly alarmed, and sprang some paces backwards, still regarding us as if undecided whether to retreat or not. But as we remained motionless, and showed no desire to approach it, it began to graze quietly with its companion. This seemed a good opportunity for getting possession of it, so, fastening one end of a long cord to a tree, I knotted the other into a running noose, which I intended to throw over the animal's head. Browsing contentedly, it moved onwards by degrees until it was near enough for Fritz, who was watching patiently, to slip the noose round its neck. Startled by the motion of his hand, it made to bound off immediately, but was pulled up so suddenly by the tightening of the cord that it dropped down as if suffocated. I hastened to loosen the cord and replace it with our own donkey's halter. Then I put my bamboo cleft stick on its nostrils, and fastened the open ends of it with a piece of string much in the same way as blacksmiths do when they have to shoe a young, vicious horse. Afterwards I tied the halter by a strong rope to a tree,

and left the prisoner to show his dissatisfaction with our treatment in whatever way he liked.

In the meantime the whole family had descended from the Nest, in order to inspect my capture. Its graceful and elegant form, so superior to that of the ass, called forth their admiration. After a while it began to jump about wildly, in the vain effort to regain its liberty; but the pain that the bamboo stick caused it brought it to its senses, and forced it to moderate its violence. In a short time it became so quiet that we went up to it without fear, and led it to the place that we used for a stable. To train the wild creature was a work of considerable difficulty; but as it promised to be a valuable beast of burden, we did not allow ourselves to be easily discouraged. When it was unusually furious I tried the experiment which the natives of South America are said to resort to under similar circumstances, and clipped its ears, these being the most sensitive parts of such animals. I found this mode of training to be most effective, and in a few weeks 'Lightfoot', as the children called our new acquisition, had profited so much by our training that we could mount it fearlessly.

While this course of education was going on, the poultry yard received considerable additions. To the delight of my wife, more than forty small chickens were added to our number, and enlivened the yard by their cheerful chirping as they hopped about in all directions.

As the rainy season or winter was drawing near, we occupied ourselves in laying in a large store of provisions of every description, so that, while the weather was unfavourable, it might not be necessary for us to continue our excursions.

One evening, as we were returning from the potato field with a cart-load of the valuable roots, it occurred to me that, if my wife would drive home the donkey, the two eldest boys and I might go as far as Oak Grove, and supply ourselves with a sack of acorns. To this she willingly agreed; so Ernest proceeded in the direction indicated, with his monkey on his shoulder, and Fritz rode forward proudly on his lightly-harnessed onagra. We had with us a couple of empty bags, which we intended to make Lightfoot carry home on his back, for as yet he could not be persuaded to assist Grizzly in drawing the cart.

When our little caravan arrived at the place, we bound the onagra to a tree, and set to work to gather as many of the fallen acorns as possible. We had not been engaged in our task for many minutes when Master Nip became somewhat excited, and sprang into a clump of low shrubs before which he had been sitting with his ears pricked up. In another minute the screaming of a bird, accompanied by the loud flapping of wings, was heard, and we concluded that a combat was going on between some denizen of the wood and our pugilistic companion.

Ernest neared the scene of the conflict, and soon cried, 'Come fast! Here is a grand nest of eggs. The bird is fighting with Nip, and can be caught if you only make haste.' Fritz ran up directly, and succeeded in securing a fine Canadian heath-fowl. In order to prevent its escape I bound its legs and wings with a cord, and Fritz held the enraged monkey, while Ernest gathered the eggs in his hat and covered them with the leaves of which the nest was partly composed, and which closely resembled those of a lily.

As the sacks were now full, it was time to think of returning to Falcon's Nest, so, having laden the onagra with our treasures, we set out. On our arrival my wife thankfully accepted our offering of eggs, and having placed them carefully in a nest, she induced one of the fowls to sit on them, as the heath-hen was too frightened to hatch them in captivity. In a short time we had the satisfaction of possessing a little brood of wild chickens, which seemed to get on very pleasantly with their tamer companions.

The lily leaves proved a source of great amusement to Franz, and their stiff, sharp points served him as most formidable weapons. When he grew wearied of trying their effect on himself and on everybody who approached him, he said, 'Come, Fritz, please, and help me. I have been trying to twist a lot of these leaves into a whip with which to drive the goats and sheep, but I am not able to manage it. I wish you would do it for me.'

His brother sat down willingly to the task, and as he was working I was struck by the toughness and flexibility of the leaves. On examining them more particularly than I had done before, I was delighted to find that we had accidentally

discovered a plant known as the *Phormium Tenax*, or New
Zealand flax plant, which serves the Indians as a good
substitute for European flax. I could not restrain my delight
at this discovery, but shouted 'Hurrah! Hurrah! Our stron-
gest desire is gratified; our greatest want supplied! Soon we
shall be clothed, if not with purple and fine linen, at least
with very welcome articles of apparel.'

My wife hurried towards me, greatly amused by my apparent excitement, and desirous of knowing what had caused it.
When I told her, her joy was as great as my own. 'For some
time I have been greatly troubled to know how we could bear
the cold of the winter without some warmer clothing,' she
said, 'and now the means are placed within my reach of
providing you with garments of every kind. Let the children
lose no time in bringing me a large quantity of these leaves,
and I shall begin work on the spot.'

She had scarcely given expression to her desire when
Ernest and Fritz mounted – one on the donkey and the other
on the buffalo – and galloped off towards Oak Wood at full
speed. While they were away I explained to my wife how far
the raw material differed in this case from the manufactured
article, and how many processes it must undergo before it
could be committed into her hands. Her disappointment was
very great, that all was not in favour of her beginning her
spinning and weaving on the spot; but I assured her the delay
would not be very serious.

After a short absence the foraging party returned, the

chargers laden with huge bunches of the plant, which the boys presented to their mother with comic gravity. They begged me at the same time to prepare it for her use without delay.

'The first thing to be done is to steep the leaves in water,' I said.

'Must the water be hot, father?' asked Jack; 'for, if so, we have no pot large enough to boil it.'

'No,' I replied; 'it only requires to be dipped in cold water, and then bleached in the air. This causes a part of the plant to decay, and the long fibrous threads can then be easily separated from the rest.'

'But do the threads themselves never rot?' questioned Fritz.

'Not unless the bleaching process is carried on too long. The thread is so tough that it needs a great deal of exposure to destroy it. But, in order to avoid all possibility of injury, we can put our flax into a pool of stagnant water instead of exposing it to the sun. The effect will be the same, but all risk of decay will be avoided.'

My wife was of opinion that, as the tropical heat of the country was so intense, it would be better to adopt the latter mode, and suggested Flamingo Marsh as a suitable place for carrying out the process. Accordingly, after having yoked the donkey to the cart, in which we piled the bunches of leaves, allowing room in the centre for Franz and Nip, we started. Fritz and Ernest followed us with shovels, pickaxes, and other tools.

Arrived at the marsh, we untied the flax and threw it into the water. We then pressed it down with large stones, so that it might be thoroughly saturated, and left it there for a fortnight. By the end of that time our anxious housewife thought it ought to be sufficiently steeped, and begged us to go and remove it out of the pond. We did so, and spread it where the sun shone warmly on it. Before evening it was quite dry, so we bundled it up again, threw it into our cart, and returned to the Nest, where we stored it until we should have time to make the wheels, reels, etc., which our chief required for her manufacture.

CHAPTER XI

THE GROTTO

H EAVY RAIN-SHOWERS, which of late fell frequently, warned us that the winter of the tropics was not far off, and, not knowing how long it might continue, we made hurried preparations for the security of a large store of provisions. Numerous excursions were made to the potato field, and as many of the prized roots brought away as we could conveniently find room for, while tapioca, cocoa-nut, and acorns filled all the sacks we could muster.

As we had no farm implements with which to prepare the ground for the reception of seed, and as, notwithstanding the many delicious productions of the island, we all missed the bread to which we had been accustomed for so long, we took the precaution of scattering wheat on the loosened soil from which we had taken the potatoes, and trusted that some of it at least would take root. As the rain that had fallen so plentifully had softened the earth, which sometimes, after a lengthened period of drought, was too hard to be dug without great labour, I transplanted several young palm trees and a number of sugar-canes to the vicinity of our dwelling.

Notwithstanding all our exertions, the change came before we were quite prepared for it. The winds raged through the

woods; the fury of the sea increased daily, until the waves
seemed like snow-capped mountains as they rolled on majestically until they broke on the beach; heavy masses of cloud
floated over the heavens, and at last burst overhead, and
torrents of rain fell night and day without intermission. Had
our Nest been as suitable for winter as for summer habitation, we should have shut ourselves in and laughed at the
storm; but, unfortunately, we soon found that the protection
which it afforded was too weak to admit of our defying the
elements. The rain entered on all sides, and the wind threatened every minute to remove our abode from its exalted
position.

As our only resource, we were compelled to withdraw to
the stall that we had erected for the accommodation of our
livestock. But what an uncomfortable retreat this proved to
be! Besides being so small as hardly to afford us packing
room, the lowing of the cows and cackling of the geese, who
seemed greatly disturbed by our intrusion, almost deafened
us; and when we attempted to light a fire, the smoke, finding
no proper outlet, rose round us in clouds, and almost stifled
us. We were therefore obliged to resign this latter comfort,
and look forward to the enjoyment of unlimited cold
victuals.

A still greater drawback than any of these, however, was
the want of forage for the animals. The rain had come so
suddenly at last that we had not had time to lay in a supply,
and we dared not divide our store of potatoes with them, lest

we ourselves should find our provisions fall short, and run the risk of perishing from hunger. It was therefore decided, in spite of the weather, to set a number of the beasts at liberty, so that they might find food for themselves. But we took care that it should be only to those which were natives of the country that freedom was accorded, as we knew they were best able to bear up under the severe cold. At the same time, it was important that they should not resume their old mode of life, so every evening Fritz and I had to brave wind and rain and go in search of them.

Although our winter quarters were of the poorest description, we yet managed to make our sojourn in them both pleasant and profitable. The writing of my journal was a most agreeable pastime both for myself and my wife, who was of great service in helping me to recall the events that had transpired since the shipwreck. The last and most useful occupation of the winter was the making of a couple of carding combs, which were necessary for combing the flax. These I formed by sticking a number of long fine nails at equal distances in a piece of tin. In order to fix them solidly in their places, I poured melted lead between them. I next nailed the bit of tin to a small board, and the machine was finished. It seemed so suitable for the purpose that my wife was tempted to begin work immediately; but as the flax had got wet with the rain, and we were unable to light a fire to dry it, she was obliged to put off her combing and carding till a more favourable season.

Who can describe our delight when, after long weeks of confinement and privation, the clouds rolled back, showing the blue sky behind them, and the sun smiled down at his own face, as he saw it reflected in every glistening drop of water, in every little running stream. All nature seemed to have been refreshed by the heavy rains. The songs of hundreds of birds that were building their nests in the neighbouring branches filled the air with melody; countless flowers covered the fertile soil, and raised their pretty heads as if inviting our admiration; the seeds which we had sown, and which we dreaded had been washed away by the floods, were shooting through the earth; and even the trees that we had transplanted were thriving vigorously.

Our task was to restore the Nest, with which the storm had made great havoc. Half of it had been carried away by the wind, and the powder and provisions that we had left in it were greatly spoiled by the rain. For several days our time was spent in rendering our domicile fit for habitation. As soon as we returned to it my wife proceeded without delay to the carding of the flax. While I went off in search of fresh forage for the cattle, the boys, in obedience to their mother's desire, stripped the leaves that we had dried; the newly-manufactured machine was then brought into requisition, and found to serve its purpose admirably.

The next article needed was a spinning-wheel, but the making of such a complicated piece of mechanism seemed to me hopeless. However, by dint of perseverance, and the application of a certain knowledge of turnery that I had gained when a boy, I managed to produce not only a wheel, but a spindle, which, though clumsy, met with my wife's warmest approval. Without taking even a day's airing after her long confinement indoors, she commenced work at once, and I set off to Tent House in order to see if it had suffered also from the fury of the tempest. I found it in even a more deplorable state than Falcon's Nest. The tent was overthrown, and a large portion of the sailcloth torn away entirely. The provisions that we had concealed there were rendered almost useless, and the vegetable garden was nearly utterly destroyed. Fortunately, the pinnace was uninjured, but the tub-boat had been battered so unmercifully by the waves that hardly a vestige of it remained.

The wholesale destruction that had been wrought on both our dwellings made me determine to provide ourselves somehow, before another winter should set in, with a commodious residence, where we could find shelter, not only for ourselves, but for our cattle.

Fritz's proposition that we should excavate a large rock, into which we could retire when we liked, seemed to me at first sight absurd and impracticable; but as, after thinking long over the matter, I could hit on no other plan, I decided at any rate to try it. First, however, we agreed to test our strength by hollowing out a cave large enough for a provision store. With this object in view, I set out one morning with Fritz and Jack, who were laden, as I was, with hammers, crowbars, pickaxes, and other similar implements.

After examining the surrounding rocks carefully, I chose

an elevated cliff that commanded a fine view on every side, and with a piece of chalk I marked on it the size of the opening that I wished to make. The work of excavation then began. During the first day we progressed but slowly, and the boys, notwithstanding their former hopefulness, became doubtful whether or not we should be able to make even a cellar. The following day, however, brought with it new strength and confidence, and as we toiled on zealously we were encouraged by finding that the stone was becoming much softer the farther we penetrated. When we had arrived at a depth of about seven feet, Jack, who was striving with a crowbar to remove a large piece of loose rock, suddenly cried out, 'Hurrah! Hurrah! I'm through!'

I approached the spot where he stood, and found, much to my amazement, that the crowbar was stuck into a small hole, and could be twisted about in every direction.

'This is very strange,' I said. 'It really seems as if the cliff were hollow, and yet I can hardly believe such to be the case.'

'Let us enlarge the hole,' suggested Fritz, 'and we shall then be able to form a more correct opinion on the matter. Through this small opening it is impossible to distinguish anything.'

As I was as eager to have my own curiosity on the subject gratified as he was to have his, I set to with a will, hammering with my pickaxe until a large opening was revealed.

'Now,' said Jack, 'if you will tie a rope round my waist, so that I may not lose my way, I shall go into the cavern and examine it, and shall be able to tell you all about it in a few minutes.'

'The experiment would be a very hazardous one, my boy,' I remarked, 'for the cave is, in all probability, full of foul air that would render you instantly insensible. The best way of testing whether this is the case or not is by fire. If a light be at once extinguished in a grotto or mine, it is a sign that the air is not fit to be breathed; so, if you gather a bundle of dried grass and twigs, I shall soon settle my doubts on the subject.'

Having lighted a few small branches, I threw them blazing into the cavern. As I expected, they went out instantly, proving that the air was most poisonous, and must be thoroughly purified before we could make our descent with safety. Thinking how this could be done, I remembered that amongst other things that we brought from the foundered vessel was a chest containing rockets and grenades which were used for giving night signals at sea, and I despatched Jack for a few of them to the tent. When he returned I threw some of the grenades into the hollow, and a noise like that of a terrible explosion succeeded. We then lighted a few rockets, and fired them in successively. They floated around like fiery dragons, disclosing to our view the mighty extent of the cavern, the sides of which glittered with diamond brilliancy. When all was again in total darkness, I kindled another bunch of grass and repeated my first experiment. This time the result was most satisfactory. The grass blazed brightly till consumed, so I knew that our descent, at least as far as the air was concerned, might be undertaken at any moment.

'Please, father, let us go down now,' begged Jack, who regarded the cave with the air of a proprietor. 'There can be no danger, since the light was not extinguished.'

'Danger takes many forms, my son,' I answered; 'and though the impure gases have escaped, there are many other things that we have cause to fear. Sometimes in caverns like this there are high precipices and deep lakes, which, in the darkness, we would not know to avoid. But if you return to the Nest and bring back with you a few candles, I am willing to gratify your desire, and begin our exploration of this wonder of nature.'

Delighted with his commission, he leaped on the buffalo, and was soon out of sight. During his absence, Fritz and I enlarged the entrance to the grotto, and cleared away the rubbish that lay before it. We had just finished when we saw Jack appearing in the distance, waving his cap and blowing a small trumpet that he usually carried at his belt. He seemed to be the bearer of some most unusual tidings. In a moment his actions were explained by the appearance of my wife, whose wonder he must have aroused greatly when he succeeded in persuading her to abandon her engrossing spinning-wheel.

'Jack tells me you have discovered the entrance to Fairy-land,' she said, when I had assisted her and Franz to alight from the rude car. 'His description of it was most glowing, and left the impression on my mind that you had seen nothing but diamond-walled chambers with golden roofs.'

'I am afraid his imagination was off again on one of its numerous excursions,' I replied. 'The grotto is hardly so gorgeous as all that, I fancy; but it is certainly very curious, and I am desirous of making a minute examination of it. Let us therefore take our candles and proceed to explore.'

We entered gravely on our expedition, I leading the band, cautiously sounding the earth on all sides, and my wife and children following, half in delighted amazement, half in fear. As we pursued our way slowly, lighted by our tapers, which were reflected brilliantly in the glittering sides of the cavern, a scene of wondrous magnificence was outspread before us, and we paused in speechless admiration. It seemed as if we were standing in the richly-illuminated saloon of some Eastern royal residence, or under the dome of some mighty temple. From the roof hung sparkling crystals of every form and brilliant hue, while from the ground rose majestic columns, forming altars, pillars, and colonnades, and giving to the place the aspect of a fairy palace pictured by the imagination. The appearance of the crystals, and the absence of any trace of humidity, led me to suspect that we were in a grotto of rock salt. On chipping off a piece of the stone and tasting it, I found my supposition to be correct. The discovery gave me sincere gratification, for the salt seemed in every way preferable to that we had before used, and we were assured of always having a plentiful supply for ourselves and our cattle, without the trouble of taking a wearisome journey to the sea-shore.

'Now, mother, what do you say to this for a winter retreat?' questioned Fritz. 'Why, living in such a gorgeous place, we could fancy ourselves princes and rulers of the earth, and could look on European powers with the eye of disdain!'

'I don't think that would add much to our comfort, or materially distress the scorned,' she replied; 'but as far as regards living here during the winter months, I would gladly remove to any spot where the rain could not penetrate.'

'I think we could establish quite a comfortable home here,' I remarked. 'The cave is so vaulted over that no storm could affect us, and it is so large that it could serve both as our storehouse and dwelling.'

As we were now convinced of the security of this underground abode, we began to plan our arrangements for rendering it fit for habitation, and many were the projects conceived for fitting it up. The children, displaying that love of change which is natural to youth, were anxious to abandon Falcon's Nest altogether; but my wife begged eagerly that it should be retained for a summer residence, and I gladly acceded to her desire. We returned to it every night, but we spent the day in making improvements in our subterranean house. In the first place, we enlarged the entrance, and fitted to it the door of the tree; for, as the latter was to be henceforth merely a sort of summer-house, it was needless to

close it up very securely, and a thin covering of bark would be sufficient to conceal the aperture from our uncivilized foes. The windows which admitted the light into the stair-case were also brought away, and fixed in holes cut in the rock. We then divided the grotto into two apartments. One of these was intended for our own accommodation, and the other for that of our livestock and the different articles which we wished to preserve. I partitioned off the right-hand division into four rooms. One of these we selected for a sitting-room, two others for sleeping apartments, and the fourth for a kitchen. In the latter I constructed a fireplace, and with a few boards built a sort of chimney that conducted the smoke through a hole in the rock. As soon as we had completed that portion of our work which was most urgent, we began to devote part of our time and attention to other matters, and only visited the grotto when we wished to deposit in it some of those belongings which we had at the Nest.

Though our lengthened sojourn in the neighbourhood of Tent House was in some ways disadvantageous, yet it led to several important discoveries. Large turtles frequently came on shore to lay their eggs in the sand, as is their custom, and by paying a little attention to the movements of the unwieldy creatures we were able to secure a large supply of these dainties without any trouble. Not content with this, how-ever, we were desirous of catching and detaining alive some of the animals themselves, so that we might use them for food whenever we wished. The idea was not long conceived till it was executed. As soon as we perceived a turtle on the beach, one of the boys cut off its retreat to the sea, and I turned it on its back; then, passing a cord through a hole in the shell, I tied it firmly to a post not far from the water. It was thus at liberty to disport itself on land or in sea; but though in the enjoyment of partial liberty, it was nevertheless our prisoner, and was ready for use whenever we required it.

One morning we were startled by a strange phenomenon out at sea. The surface of the water for a considerable space foamed and boiled as if a volcano were at work below it, and now and again what seemed like a brilliant shower of sparks issued from it and glittered in the sunlight. Countless sea-birds floated like a cloud over this sparkling wave-mass, screaming and chattering as if in expectation of prey. As the moving body approached the coast steadily, various were our surmises regarding it. My wife was of opinion that it was a sandbank, and that the motion which we were sure we perceived was merely the result of our imagination. Fritz thought the wonderful commotion was caused by a subterranean burning mountain. Ernest suggested the probability of it being some unknown monster floating with its back on a level with the sea. After a few minutes' observation it became evident to me that what was the cause of so much astonishment and surmise was a herring shoal entering the bay.

Seeing such a favourable opportunity for providing ourselves with a quantity of wholesome provisions, I decided to

organize a fishery at once. Fritz took up his position in the water, and so thick was the shoal that it was only necessary for him to drop in a basket and draw it out full of fish. When he threw the herrings on the sand, Ernest and Jack cut them open and cleaned them, and my wife rubbed them well with salt. As the work of packing them required most skill, I took it upon myself, and placed them between layers of salt in the few remaining casks which we had. When all were filled, I covered the barrels with leaves, and nailed boards securely down on them; then, placing them on the car, we transported them to our winter storehouse in the grotto.

The appearance of our kitchen garden at Tent House afforded us at this time great pleasure. In spite of the apparent wholesale destruction that the rain-storm had wrought in it, an abundant crop of vegetables of various sorts rewarded the labours of my wife. In addition to beans, lettuces, peas, etc., the melons and cucumbers were laden with fruit, the sugar-canes were in a prosperous condition, and the maize was more than a foot high. The flourishing state of our garden made us so hopeful that we set off to the cornfield in order to see if our toil there had been equally productive. What was our surprise to find a most luxuriant crop, for the most part ready for reaping! But our harvest treasures had not failed to attract a host of destructive animals, whose traces were everywhere visible. On the approach of the dogs, whole flocks of birds took wing immediately; numbers of quails darted hither and thither, frightened by our presence; and even several kangaroos hopped swiftly away.

We now returned to Falcon's Nest, intending to begin the harvest in a couple of weeks, as we thought the whole crop would, in all probability, be ripe by that time. Accordingly, when that period had elapsed, we fastened the entrance to our dwelling, and made everything as secure as possible; harnessed the cow and buffalo to the car, in which we had placed a number of scythes, hooks, and other implements that we expected would serve to lighten our toil; loaded Grizzly and Lightfoot with the provisions which we had packed in small hampers, and started.

When we reached the river that flowed between us and that part of the island where our cornfield lay, we were surprised to find that the bridge by which we usually crossed had been washed away during the recent storm, and that in order to reach the other side it was necessary to advance far northward, through a district which we had not yet

LOUIS RHEAD.

explored, until we arrived at the source. For some time our progress was so slow that we became quite despondent, and feared we should never be able to overcome the many difficulties that beset us. Long grass and clinging plants obstructed us at every step, and in some places the shrubs grew so thickly that we were obliged to hew a path through them. At last we emerged from the almost impenetrable jungle, and reached a comparatively open plain, where here and there grew little thickets of low bushes, covered with some white substance.

'How funny to see snow in summer,' said Franz, highly delighted with the novelty. 'Come, father, and let us have a good game of snowballing; only, please, don't put it down my back.'

'Oh, Franz, what a goose you are, to be sure! Fancy seeing snow when the sun is shining! That white stuff is sago, such as father brought home some time ago,' said Jack, in a most instructive manner.

'Not so fast, my young teacher,' I interrupted, while the rest laughed at the simple blunders of the children. 'You were quite right when you said it was not snow with which the trees are covered, but you were quite wrong when you asserted it to be sago. As far as I can judge at this distance, it is cotton, and those are specimens of the cotton plant which grows abundantly in America.'

On reaching one of the clumps of shrubs I found my surmise to be correct. What caused the bushes to present such a white appearance was that the pods, having arrived at maturity, had burst, and the down with which they were filled had partially escaped, and clothed the branches with a snowy mantle. We collected a quantity of this valuable commodity, and my wife filled her pocket with the seed, intending to raise a small cotton plantation in the neighbourhood of the Nest. Our cotton harvest reaped, we prosecuted our march, and soon gained a considerable elevation, from which we were able to obtain a wide view of the surrounding country. Trees of every description grew luxuriantly on all sides; from their branches hung tempting fruits, which afforded us welcome refreshment; under their shade flowed little murmuring streams, along whose banks grew flowers of every hue, which, fanned by the west wind, nodded their heads to us as if in welcome, while the soft grass with which the soil was carpeted provided an enjoyable meal for our cattle. As we were all enchanted with the beauty and fertility of the spot, we decided to make it one of our future halting-places, and to establish a little farmyard on the summit of the hill, to which we could remove a number of our livestock. This idea we had had for some time in contemplation, as of late the increase of our animals had been so great as to cause us to fear they might become a burden to us; and we resolved to form in the open country a sort of colony, in the hope that its members would thrive and propagate their species without entailing on us the trouble of feeding and tending them. Hitherto a suitable situation for the farmery had been lacking, but that want was now supplied, and we determined to begin to build on the morrow.

CHAPTER XII

GATHERING THE HARVEST

THE FOLLOWING day, having selected what seemed the most convenient spot for the construction of the stalls, we commenced to work, and, before nightfall, had erected a good-sized hut, which promised to provide comfortable accommodation for as many of our cattle as we could afford to lodge at a distance from our dwelling. Round the inside walls, which were built of wild vines and flexible reeds, at a distance of a couple of feet from the ground, we set up a number of racks. These we filled with the favourite food of the various animals, and we expected that thus they would be enticed to return every evening to the shelter of their stall. It was arranged that the fodder should be renewed every day until our winged and four-footed colonists should become habituated to their new abode.

In peeling off the bark of some of the neighbouring trees, to obtain material for roofing, we were fortunate enough to discover both gum mastic and turpentine. My gratification on finding them was extreme, for I knew that, having them, I was furnished with a good substitute for pitch, with which I could overlay my boat, and which would serve many other useful purposes.

For the not less welcome discovery of cinnamon we were indebted to the goats. Observing them rolling on the ground, and chewing some chips of a particular bark with evident satisfaction, we were led to examine what they appeared to relish so much, and found it to be this highly-prized spice.

Next day I desired Ernest and Fritz to return to the Nest to look after the animals, and also to bring with them a number of hens and ducks, sheep and goats, with which to stock the farmery. While they were executing this commission, Jack and I set out on a pilgrimage, accompanied by Topsy. In doing so, we had two objects in view: one was to make ourselves better acquainted with the surrounding district; the other was to search for cocoa-nuts, tapioca, potatoes, or any other root or fruit which we could use for food. Having traversed a wide marsh, we reached a lake that lay glistening in the sunlight like a sheet of silver. On its banks grew wild rice in abundance, from which an immense number of birds rose with a great noise on our approach. I gathered a few handfuls of the rice, in order to ascertain whether, on being cooked, it was fit to be eaten or not.

A little farther on we entered a small grove, and here Nip made a discovery that laid us under lasting obligation to him. As he rode along, cavalierly mounted on Topsy's back, he suddenly sprang to the ground, and, making his way through the long grass, began to devour something which, from his grimaces, I judged to be pleasant to his palate. It turned out to be some splendid strawberries on which he was feasting royally. The delicious fruit grew here in wild profusion. After satiating ourselves, we filled the pannier that Nip always carried with the berries, and covered them carefully, lest the porter should be tempted to help himself on the way. These I intended to take as a treat to my wife and the boys.

As we continued our journey along the banks of the lake, I observed a number of beautiful black swans floating about proudly, and now and again gazing admiringly at the reflection of their graceful forms in the unruffled water. Their appearance pleased me so much that I could not find in my heart to interfere with them, though I should gladly have been the possessor of one of the splendid creatures. But Topsy's admiration was not ardent enough to overcome her love of slaughter. She dashed into the lake, but before she had reached the birds her attention was distracted from them by the appearance of a curious-looking animal that had escaped my notice before. She seized it, and was about to tear it in pieces when I prevented her. The prize measured about a foot and a half in length; it was covered with short brown hair, and had a bill like a duck's. Both its fore and hind feet were webbed, and the latter were provided with strong spurs. For some time I considered the animal attentively without being able to come to any conclusion regarding it, for it was utterly different from anything I had ever seen, and my knowledge of natural history gave me no clue to its identification. At last I remembered a description of a curious creature called the duck-billed platypus that I had read of a few days previously in one of the captain's books, and I recognized it to be one of the species. It was first discovered on a lake in New Zealand, and has puzzled naturalists not a little. As it was such a rarity, I decided to take it home, and try to preserve it if possible.

Bearing our trophy, we returned to the hut, and arrived just in time to receive Ernest and Fritz, who had performed their journey without adventure, and had brought back the animals that I required. Having lodged these in their newly-erected abode, we retired to rest.

As soon as we had partaken of breakfast next morning, we filled the stable racks with fresh fodder, tied the sheep and goats to posts at the entrance to the stall, so that they might not wander away during our absence, and left the spot, which the boys had named Forest Farm, to proceed in the direction opposite to that which Jack and I had chosen on the previous day. The first thing that attracted our observation was a troop of monkeys, by whom our approach was greeted with loud cries and a shower of fir cones. On examining some of the cones, I found they had a very pleasant taste, and contained a great deal of oil, so I told the boys to make an abundant provision of them, as it was very probable they could be employed for some useful purpose. As we pursued our route in an easterly direction towards the mouth of the river, my wife observed several large dark objects floating on the water; but before she could form any opinion regarding them a long line of trees obstructed her view. In the course of a few minutes we reached a point where the river was again visible, and she then attracted my attention to a large unshapely head that appeared above the water, and that was turned in the direction of the shore. After gazing at us steadily for a moment or two, the animal seemed to resolve on cultivating a closer acquaintance, for it swam rapidly forward until it reached the strand; then it halted, standing partly in the river, partly on land. Thinking that an encounter with it would be by no means to be desired, we retreated slowly, and should have escaped, had not Topsy and Bill been aroused by its extraordinary aspect, and rushed towards it, bent on attack. With a terrible growl of mingled defiance and anger, the brute emerged altogether from the water, and I then saw that it was a hippopotamus, or river horse, with which we had to deal.

'As I shall likely have some trouble in getting rid of this visitor,' I said to my family, 'it is better for you to make for that rugged eminence which you see at some little distance. If the animal attempts to follow you, which I don't think it will, run in a zigzag course, and you will escape easily.'

My wife and children obeyed reluctantly, for they would have much preferred to remain with me, but I insisted on their departure. I then stationed myself opposite the animal, and, aiming carefully at his eye, fired two shots. Whether it was owing to my own excitement or to some movement on the part of the hippopotamus I know not, but my balls only grazed the creature's neck and roused him to fury. With an angry snort he rushed after me as I made for the hill, which the others had safely reached. For a while I kept far in front, but at last I felt my strength giving way, and I saw that my pursuer was gaining upon me. On I rushed madly, fearing every moment to be overtaken, and hardly heeding whither I went; closer and closer came the enraged monster; every moment I could hear his sullen growls more distinctly, and my hopes of escape had grown very faint indeed, when suddenly I tripped over a large stone, and fell flat to the earth. Before I could regain my feet the brute was within a yard of me, and I thought my last hour had come. But brave Bill saw my danger, and bounded towards the hippopotamus, thus distracting his attention from me. Taking advantage of the respite offered me, I ran with the swiftness of despair until I had gained the summit of the hill. When the animal attempted the pursuit again he was deterred by the steepness of the eminence, so, turning away with a dissatisfied growl, he plunged amid the brushwood, that crackled and broke beneath his heavy tread. In a few minutes he emerged from his place of concealment, and stood looking round as if in search of something on which to vent his wrath; then marched forward at a stately pace, and entered a thicket that bordered the wood.

As soon as I had recovered from my fright our interrupted journey was continued. But we had not gone far when a low grunt was again heard, and at the same instant I perceived, standing not far from us, the hippopotamus, who evidently

desired to renew the encounter. As it was useless to think of
resorting to flight this time, on account of the long grass
which would have tripped us at every step, our only plan was
to face the enemy boldly. Raising our guns, we all three fired
at the same moment. When the smoke cleared away we saw
the hippopotamus standing motionless, and we feared that
our balls had failed to reach the mark; but ere we had time to
give expression to our fear he tottered and fell dead to the
ground. Having measured the carcass, which we found to be
fourteen feet in length and five in height, we removed the
skin, for, as I explained to the boys, it was, owing to its
toughness, particularly suited for making harness and whips.

Continuing our march, we reached the bridge without
further adventure. We crossed it, and turned towards Monkey Wood. As we entered it the last rays of the sun were
gilding the tops of the palm trees, and without delay we
made our necessary preparations for passing the night here.
As soon as we had secured the beasts to a neighbouring tree,
and lighted a fire large enough to burn for several hours, we
retired under cover of the tent.

Next morning we set out for Prospect Hill, which lay in
the vicinity of Cape Disappointment, and reached it ere the
sun was high in the heavens. Quite close to it was our
cornfield. The boys were eager to begin to reap on the spot,
but as the crop would not suffer by being allowed to remain
uncut for a day or two longer, it seemed to me better first to
erect a small tent similar to that at Forest Farm, in which we

could pass the nights securely while the harvest lasted, and which would likewise serve as a halting-place whenever we might make excursions along the coast. Owing to the difficulty that we had in procuring building materials, our work progressed more slowly than I had expected; but in a few days it was completed to our universal satisfaction, and the reaping was commenced.

The amount of corn and wheat which the potato ground had produced was very abundant, and promised not only plenty of flour to last until the following autumn, but also enough seed with which to renew the crop.

The scythes that we had brought with us were now called into requisition, and until noon the work of mowing progressed vigorously. After dinner, instead of again applying ourselves to the scythes, we spread a large sailcloth on the earth, and having laid a few armfuls of the corn that we had already cut on it, we threshed it with sticks until every grain was separated from the straw. After that we shook it through a sieve, so as to clean it thoroughly, and then packed it in bags. Every day for a week the same programme was gone through, and at the end of that time we turned the cattle on the field, according to the ancient Eastern custom, and let them glean what was left.

Now that the farm produce was gathered in, the boys were anxious that I should reward them for their labour by allowing them to make a short journey farther inland in search of curiosities. Though desirous to grant their request,

I was obliged to refuse it for the present, for I had in contemplation a task which I required their aid to enable me to perform.

For some time I had been on the look-out for a certain tree, the bark of which I had read would make a canoe such as the Indians use. Since I had been located at Prospect Hill, I had discovered that of which I had so long been in search. In height and foliage the tree bore a strong resemblance to an oak, and its fruit, though smaller, was in many respects similar to the acorn, but its bark was peculiarly tough, and as light as cork. After having selected one that seemed most suitable for the purpose we had in view, Ernest and I fastened to its lower branches the rope ladder that we had brought from Falcon's Nest. Having mounted on this to the top of the trunk, Fritz sawed through the bark above until he came to the wood, and I performed the same operation at the base. We then cut out a narrow strip from the top to the bottom, and by means of wooden wedges, which we inserted very carefully, we separated the covering in one solid piece. The most difficult part of the work was yet to be performed. Having laid the moist bark on the grass, I proceeded to give it the required shape. With my axe I cut a slit in each of the ends, lapped the separated parts over each other, and nailed them firmly together, so as to form a point at each extremity. As it was now widened too much in the middle, we tied strong ropes round it, and brought it to its proper shape. Then it was placed in the sun to dry; but much yet remained to be done before the boat could be looked on as finished. In order to provide it with ribs, I made a short excursion in search of some branches of a peculiar tree, called by the Indians 'firewood'. When I had found them I cut them into the proper size and form, and fixed them in the canoe. I also was fortunate enough to find a resinous tree, from which a sort of pitch issued that soon became hard when exposed to the sun, and that was much to be preferred to the turpentine and gum mastic for coating the boat. My wife and Franz collected a considerable quantity of this substance, as they thought it would answer many useful purposes.

On the following morning we placed the canoe and corn-sacks on the car and set out for Tent House; but by the time we had arrived at Forest Farm we felt greatly fatigued, so we passed the night there. The cattle were in a very prosperous condition, and showed by their improved appearance that they had not failed to avail themselves of the rich grass that grew around them, as well as of the fodder that the boys had taken care to provide for them every day.

Next day we reached Tent House, and as soon as we had attended to some urgent business we resumed the completion of our boat. A mast, sail, rudder, and movable seats were added to it. To the outside of the bulwarks I attached some bladders filled with air. These rendered the canoe very buoyant, and also greatly facilitated the launching of it. A few days later we removed to Falcon's Nest, and found that during our absence the cow had presented us with a fine male calf. As each of the older boys was already provided with a pet, I presented the new arrival to Franz, and accompanied the gift with the promise to train it for his use. The child was delighted with the animal, and thanked me warmly for it. 'I shall take the best possible care of it,' he said, 'and I shall feed it every day myself, and give it everything I think it would like to eat. I mean to call it "Growler" too, for the only sound it makes is a low, growling one, which is anything but musical, and which shows the beast has a temper of its own.'

'The idea of christening the calf is a very good one,' said I, 'and I think Jack would not do wrong if he adopted it. The donkey and onagra have already been designated, and if the buffalo also bore a name peculiar to himself all confusion would henceforth be avoided.'

'Three cheers, then, for the noble "Storm", for that is the name I intend bestowing on my charger,' shouted Jack, acting on my suggestion with his customary impetuosity. 'When he is angry he is as wild as any storm, so I think I have called him by a very appropriate title. I shall also take on me to christen the puppies, although they don't belong to me. Let them be called "Brown" and "Fawn", in accordance with their different colours.'

This was unanimously agreed to, so henceforth the young dogs were known by the names that Jack had bestowed on them.

The next two months were taken up in finishing our cavernous dwelling, and in trying to render it as comfortable as possible. The floors of the bed-chambers we first of all covered with clay, and then overlaid with a large quantity of small pebbles, so as to prevent dampness; while for our sitting-room we manufactured a carpet, which, though devoid of beauty, added greatly to our comfort, and pleased us exceedingly. It was made by covering a sailcloth with a thick layer of wool and goat's hair; over this we poured a cement made of isinglass and gum. We then rolled up the cloth and beat it for a considerable time. When it was dry another coating of wool and gum was added, and soon we had an admirable floorcloth.

One morning I awoke earlier than was my custom, but being unwilling to arouse my family before the usual hour, I lay quietly in my hammock and tried to reckon what length of time had elapsed since we had been cast on the island on which we now were. To my surprise I found that the following day would be the anniversary of our arrival. I immediately decided that this important day should not pass without being celebrated in the best way in our power, and we spent it in feasting and games.

CHAPTER XIII

THE STRANDED WHALE

A LMOST BEFORE we realized it, autumn had come and gone, and again the rainy season was upon us. With plenty of food laid in store, we retired into the grotto, and looked out on a scene of lightning, thunder, and torrential rain. While the storm raged we could not help thinking of the discomforts and privations we had endured during the last rainy season, and contrasting them thankfully with the comforts that were now at our disposal. But though so much time had been spent on the fitting up of our dwelling, and though we had done so much to render it habitable, we were astonished to find what a lot of things must be done before we could sit down and rest with the feeling that its arrangements were complete. Want of sufficient light was a serious drawback, for that which was admitted through the three windows was very dim indeed. This defect, however, was remedied by means of a few candles, which we fastened in wooden sconces round the walls, and which, as well as illumining, added much to the beauty of our apartment by their bright reflection in the glittering crystal. Tables, chairs, movable stairs, shelves, and other things without which the house felt empty, had to be manufactured. One small room was fitted up as a forge and carpenter's workroom, and in it were placed a turner's lathe, a chest of tools, some copper and gunsmith's implements, an anvil, a pair of bellows, hammers, and other things suited for the trades with which we professed an acquaintance.

On the shelves that we had nailed up round the sitting-room we ranged our stock of books, which consisted of some volumes of natural history, a few mathematical and theological works, several grammars and dictionaries in various languages, and some entertaining books of travel.

An immense chest, which hitherto we had not taken time to open, thinking it contained nothing of importance, was produced from a recess in the cave in which it had been lodged some time before by Ernest, and I was requested to satisfy the curiosity of all by prying into its contents. On doing so, we found ourselves in possession of many articles of which we knew not how to dispose in our present circumstances. Writing-tables, mirrors, marble-topped consoles, and other luxurious pieces of furniture were one by one brought to light and handed over to our housekeeper, who distributed them amongst our apartments, to the intense delight of the boys.

All this time lightning, wind, and rain threatened to devastate the land. By degrees, however, the storm abated, and loud 'hurrahs' greeted the first ray of sunshine that struggled through the heavy masses of clouds behind which it had been so long hidden.

The change in the weather was, as I anticipated, the signal for the boys to suggest an excursion, and I willingly agreed. We chose the route along the coast. Instead of keeping to the usual path, the boys preferred to clamber over the rocks, and as they proceeded they called my attention to a large black mass of something lying near a small island out in the bay. As the telescope was not powerful enough to enable me to distinguish with certainty what it was, I resolved to make use of the canoe, and cross the intervening water, in order to get a closer view of it. Ernest and Jack accompanied me. As we approached the strange object, various were our conjectures regarding it. One thought it was an overturned boat; another a huge rock that had been dislodged by the waves, and cast on this jutting point of land. I inclined to the belief that it was a stranded whale, and on disembarking I found I was not mistaken. Soon we were measuring the animal and reckoning the amount of oil it was likely to afford us. As we had left home without the necessary appliances for dissecting the marine monster, however, we were obliged to leave it as we found it, with the determination to return on the following day and secure the blubber and baleen.

On our way back the current was strongly against us, and the boys found working at the oars a most laborious task. They pulled like men, but our progress was very slow, notwithstanding their efforts.

'I wonder,' said Ernest, 'if it would not be possible to invent some contrivance which would fill the place of a miniature steam-engine, and propel the boat smoothly over the water without entailing such dreadful work on the rowers? I think, father, you surely could hit upon some plan for lightening our toil.'

'You have more confidence in my ingenuity than I have myself,' I replied; 'but I shall do my best to meet your wishes. If you could find me a large iron wheel, I believe I could make a sort of paddle by which the canoe could be moved forward. I shall make the attempt, at any rate, the first day I get time.'

When we had landed, and I had told my wife of the whale, and of our intention to return next day to the island, she expressed a desire to go with us, as she was anxious to see the huge animal before it was cut up. Next morning, therefore, we furnished the boat with tools and provisions, and also placed a few tubs on board. As the sea had become quite calm, we had no difficulty in anchoring close to the colossal creature.

The whale measured about eighty feet in length, more than forty in diameter, and was several tons weight.

Before commencing to dissect it we took off our ordinary clothing, and donned some coarser garments which my wife had prudently advised us to bring with us. Fritz and Jack then climbed on the animal's back, and strutted about in keen enjoyment of their novel position. On examining the head they were amazed to find that it formed fully a third of the entire carcass, while the eyes were no larger than those of an ox. I showed them how to remove the baleen, or whale-

bone, several hundred pieces of which were on each side of the upper jaw. This baleen is a series of thin, horny plates, which cover the whole upper part of the mouth, and which supply the place of teeth, for the whale differs from other animals in not chewing its food. From the flanks we cut off a large quantity of blubber, and placed it in the tubs; and from the interior of the carcass I procured the liver and some portions of the intestines, which I intended to convert into bags for containing the oil. I also took some pieces of the tough skin, which was about three-quarters of an inch thick, but the larger part of the dead creature I left to the birds that were hovering around, undaunted by our presence, and that were evidently waiting for a chance to carry off part of our prize. As evening approached we transported our valuable though unsavoury cargo to the canoe, and rowed towards the Fortress, as the boys had named the grotto.

The next morning we proceeded to convert the blubber into oil. Owing to the disgusting odour that exhaled from the cauldron in which the blubber was placed after the first running had been obtained from it, we had great difficulty in carrying on the work. My wife shut herself in the cave, thinking thus to avoid the insupportable smell, but it penetrated even to the innermost chambers, and she was obliged to come out at last, as in the close room it was even more unbearable than in the open air.

By pressing the blubber we obtained as much pure oil as filled two large tubs, and then, by the aid of a brisk fire, we extracted ten skinfuls of ordinary train oil. During the performance of this operation we were unable to taste food, for the smell of our clothes and hands was so nauseous as to render us quite sick. We lodged this new treasure as far from the Fortress as we could, and only kept a small quantity of it in our dwelling at once.

The promise that I had made to construct an apparatus that would likely lessen the labour of rowing the boat was not forgotten, and as soon as the boys supplied me with the necessary wheels I set about it at once. The machine consisted of a pair of revolving paddles, to which I attached floats made of whalebone. These wheels were made to rotate in the water by a small engine, which I perfected after numerous failures and infinite trouble. At sight of the contrivance the delight of the boys knew no bounds. In order to satisfy them, I had to put out to sea and make a short tour to test the success of the job. I was glad to find that it exceeded my most sanguine expectations.

My wife's anxiety at this time regarding our stock of linen, which was diminishing rapidly, led me to attempt to make a loom, on which she could weave some necessary fabrics for clothing. The attention which I had paid, when a boy, to the mechanism of such machines was now of the greatest help to me, and I turned out a loom that, I flattered myself, could hardly be surpassed in either form or finish. I had kept the fact that I was engaged on it a secret from my wife, so when I brought it forth and presented it to her she hardly knew how to express her surprise and gratitude.

The success that I had achieved encouraged me to renewed exertions, and I supplied the household with many articles which I had hitherto deemed it impossible for any but a proper turner to produce. I also increased our worldly goods by a few baskets, the want of which had often been felt when we wished to carry seeds, fruit, or such like from one place to another. The first were made with common osier, and were so rough and unshapely that I despaired of ever making even a passable one, but after many efforts I turned out a few of tolerable appearance.

One bright morning, as we were all assembled on the balcony chatting hopefully about our future prospects, I noticed Fritz gazing fixedly towards a little hillock which lay between the grotto and Falcon's Nest. Suddenly he exclaimed, 'What on earth can that be that I see in the distance, surrounded by a cloud of dust, and that seems to be approaching us? I have been watching it for some minutes without being able to make out what it is. Sometimes it looks like a coil of thick rope lying on the ground; sometimes like the straight trunk of a young tree rising out of the earth.'

I took the telescope and directed it towards the point indicated. As I looked, a cry of alarm escaped me.

'Hide in the grotto as quickly as you can,' I said to my wife, 'and keep Franz there with you. You, boys, load your guns, and prepare for a serious encounter. A terrible serpent is close to us.'

As the boys disappeared I continued to survey the monster, but seeing that it was without doubt advancing towards us, I too retired to the cavern, and stopped up all the openings except one, from which we could see without being seen. The fearful reptile trailed its enormous body along the river's bank, only pausing now and again as if in doubt what route to pursue, or as if conscious of some hostile presence, and hesitating whether or not to flee. On it came, however, straight towards the grotto.

Thinking the moment for action had arrived, Ernest raised his gun and fired, and his example was followed by Fritz and Jack. It may have been that their hands were rendered unsteady by excitement, or that the scales of the monster were impervious to bullets. At any rate the dis-charge only caused the animal to raise its head as if surprised, and glide swiftly towards the marsh, where it disappeared. A universal expression of relief followed its departure, and the children congratulated each other on having been preserved from such imminent peril.

'I am afraid the danger is not altogether past,' I said, after I had listened for a few moments to their remarks. 'It is probable that the boa will lie in wait near here for some days, and we must exercise the greatest caution. Let none of you ever leave the grotto, or remove the boards with which the doors and windows are fastened, until we have convincing proof that our enemy is really gone.'

For three days we were in a state of siege. The agitation which was visible amongst the fowls, and the evident uneasiness of the pigeons, which cooed incessantly as they flew from rock to rock, showed us that our dreaded enemy was at hand. So, although the diminution of our store of victuals made us feel anxious, we still remained within our fortress. Every hour rendered our situation more critical. On the fourth day, seeing nothing but starvation in prospect for the cattle, with whom prudence forbade us to share our small quantity of provisions, I determined to turn them out of their stalls, and drive them up towards the source of the river, in the opposite direction to the marsh, where we still supposed the boa to be concealed. Fritz begged to be allowed to undertake the hazardous duty of leading them to the chosen spot, and as I knew he could take better care of himself than any of the others, I granted his request. Having slipped nooses over the heads of the cow, ass, and buffalo, I gave the reins into his hands, so that they might not rush about at will; but I warned him, in case of the appearance of the serpent, to let them go, and make good his own escape.

Ernest and Jack stood at the window with their loaded guns, in readiness to fire should they see any necessity, and I took up my position on the balcony, from whence I could obtain a view of the whole district.

Fritz mounted his onagra, and was just about to start when Grizzly took advantage of the loosened rein, and started off at full gallop, capering and kicking up his heels, in evident enjoyment of his freedom. Though we could not help laughing at his grotesque gambols, we yet felt the danger he was incurring, for he was nearing the marsh in his mad course. We attempted to call him back, but he only looked round in response to our shouts, and then dashed on again, regardless of our signals, and apparently determined to enjoy his frolic.

As the poor animal arrived near the lair of the serpent, we suddenly saw a terrible head raised above the reeds. The donkey perceived his danger, but, instead of fleeing from it, stood as if fascinated, and uttered a plaintive groan. The boa approached steadily with hungry jaws distended. Still Grizzly held his ground, and gazed at the monster, which the next minute wound its long, scaly body round him, and suffocated him in the horrible embrace. We shuddered as we looked on the fearful sight, and a cry of heartfelt sorrow at the death of their favourite escaped the boys.

'Had we not better fire now?' asked Ernest. 'The hateful beast must not escape, and this is likely as good an opportunity as we shall have of getting at it.'

'Let us wait for a little,' I replied; 'although the reptile seems to be regardless of everything but its prey just now, who can tell whether, if we advanced more closely to it, or turned our guns on it, we might not attract its attention to ourselves? We cannot benefit the poor donkey now, for his life is already extinct; so let us have patience till the victim is swallowed. When glutted with food, the boa may be attacked without danger.'

'Surely the vicious beast will not swallow Grizzly at a mouthful,' remarked Jack, shocked at the thought of seeing his friend thus summarily disposed of.

'It is a known fact that serpents have no teeth with which to rend their prey; so skin, flesh, bones, and all go to form their meal. They crush and squeeze the animal's body till it is reduced to the proper size for swallowing whole.'

As I spoke, the boa was kneading its victim into a shapeless mass, of which one could distinguish nothing but the mangled and bloody head. Horrified by the spectacle, my wife retired with Franz to the sitting-room, and I and the older boys waited in expectation of the moment when, gorged with its prey, the reptile would be in our power. Having covered the carcass over with slimy saliva, and stretched itself out at full length in front of it, it commenced its repast. By degrees the legs and body of the ass disappeared within its distended jaws. When all was consumed but the head, the reptile's hunger seemed to be satisfied, and it rolled over, perfectly helpless. This was the moment for which I had been waiting. Advancing to within about twenty paces of where the enemy lay, glaring at us with eyes glistening with impotent rage, but completely disarmed, I called to the boys to fire. A triple report was heard in answer to my call. The serpent writhed convulsively, its scaly body contracted, a quiver ran through its frame, and the next instant it lay dead at our feet.

Jack, who wished to perform some heroic deed, and who

hardly knew how he was to do it, fired his pistol at the boa as a parting salute. The effect was electric. The tail seemed galvanized; it twisted round once or twice, then flew up suddenly, and hit Jack such a smart blow on the chest that it knocked him down. In a second he had regained his feet, and, thinking the creature was alive, he ran off at the top of his speed. It was with difficulty I could persuade him that there was no cause for alarm, and that he might return, feeling perfectly safe.

The shout of victory that we raised on the death of the dreaded serpent told my wife of the result of our attack, and she came forth from her place of concealment to congratulate us on having rid the neighbourhood of such a dangerous visitor.

'What is to be done with the skin of the beast?' asked Jack, who had by this time recovered from his fright. 'I think we ought to stuff it, and keep it in remembrance of the most dangerous adventure we have yet met with. We could hang it above the entrance to our dwelling, and the sight of such a doorkeeper would make the savages think twice before entering.'

'Could we not eat the huge thing?' questioned Franz, whom our late lack of provisions had rather alarmed. 'I'm sure it would make roasts and stews enough to last us for a fortnight.'

'Oh, Franz, what a stupid boy you are!' laughed Fritz. 'Fancy eating the flesh of a venomous creature like that! You must be very tired of the world when you propose such a thing.'

'His proposition is by no means so foolish as you imagine,' I interrupted. 'The boa is not venomous, and even if it were, we could eat the flesh of the body without running any risk, as it is only the fangs and glands that contain the poison. In some countries a liquid preparation called snake soup is made from these reptiles, and is highly esteemed for invalids. But though it could be used as food, we had better try and preserve it as a curiosity and trophy of our victory.'

'How shall we ever get the skin removed?' asked Fritz. 'As we wish to preserve it, it would be a pity to cut it, and yet I see no other means of getting it off.'

'I can put you in the way of overcoming the difficulty,' I replied. 'You have only to make an incision round the neck, and turn back the skin a little; then fasten the upper side of this skin to a branch by cords, and the under part by wooden pins to the ground. When it is thus firmly secured, harness the oxen to the head, and let them draw the body gently out of its covering.'

'Oh, father, how absurd!' said Fritz. 'Why do you make fun of us? Please tell us really some way of removing the skin.'

'My dear child, I am giving you the best advice I can,' was my reply. 'If you adopt the plan which I have suggested, I shall be astonished if you do not find it to succeed.'

Thus assured the children obeyed my orders, and soon the skin lay empty and whole, ready for being preserved.

'Now, please, what must we fill it with?' asked Fritz. 'Would not cotton do very well?'

'It would certainly, if you had it, but I fear you are mistaken if you think your mother will give up what we gathered for her,' I answered. 'She will devote it to a much more useful purpose than snake-stuffing, and moss will do you equally well.'

On hearing this, Jack and Franz ran off to collect a quantity, and Ernest and Fritz, under my directions, proceeded to salt the inside of the skin, and sprinkle it with ashes. This done, they stuffed it tightly with moss, sewed on the head, and then endeavoured to place it in a characteristic posture.

This was a task of no small difficulty; but at last we got it wound round the forked stem of a tree that we had cut for the purpose. The head, which was raised about eight feet from the ground, was thrown forward, as if the creature was about to strike a victim, and the extended tongue was dyed with the juice of the Indian fig. In the absence of glass eyes, I replaced them with little balls of gypsum, varnished with fish glue.

The appearance of the beast was so lifelike and natural, when we had done with it, that the dogs never passed it without whining, and the cattle were so terrified on seeing it for the first time that, until it was dry, we were obliged to lead them to another field than that in which they usually pastured. When it had been long enough exposed to the sun, we placed it at the entrance to a little apartment that we had lately converted into a museum.

CHAPTER XIV

EXPLORING THE SAVANNAH

O NE EVENING I proposed to the boys, who had of late frequently besought me to extend my explorations and give them an opportunity of meeting with some stirring adventure, that on the following day we should undertake a journey to the Savannah, or low-lying district of the island. My suggestion was received with enthusiastic applause. Such was the excitement of the young people over the contemplated excursion, that sleep refused to visit them, and they tossed restlessly on their beds, sighing for the light of morning.

Day had scarcely dawned when they got up and commenced to array themselves in what they called their sportsmen's suits – suits of which excessive ugliness was the chief feature.

Having filled the game-bags with what remained after we had partaken of breakfast, as well as with some choice dainties which my wife insisted on putting up for us, we took leave of her and Franz, both of whom prudence forbade me to allow to accompany us, and turned our faces towards that unknown land lying on the eastern side of Prospect Hill. Our dogs accompanied us. For a short distance we followed the river as it wound its tortuous course through meadow, grove, and thicket; but finding our progress to be very slow, we struck out in another direction. In proportion as we advanced, the country became more arid and barren, until at last there seemed nought before us but a never-ending desert, whose monotonous stretch was unrelieved by even a withered shrub or tuft of scorched grass. Not a vestige of vegetation was to be seen; not a drop of water could be found with which to moisten our parched lips; not even a friendly rock rose up to offer us shelter from the burning heat. At last, however, after a slow march of two hours' duration we reached a hill, the top of which was crowned with olive trees, and the sides clothed with clustering shrubs. The boys would willingly have remained on this spot till midnight, but as we were obliged to return home that day, owing to the scant supply of provisions that we had brought with us, and as I was anxious to penetrate a little farther, I only allowed them time to satisfy their hunger. The victuals with which our knapsacks were filled were greedily partaken of, and we quenched our thirst by sucking a few pieces of sugar-cane that Fritz had wisely put in his bag.

As we proceeded, the aspect of the country changed entirely. The soil was covered with shrubs and brushwood, which served as a hiding-place for many beasts, whose loud growls reached our ears as we passed, while birds of every description seemed here to have their lodging-place. By degrees the shrubbery grew thinner, and the green pasture lands spread out in front of us; far away another stretch of golden sand was visible. The children forgot their recent fatigue in contemplating the unusual sight of flat green meadows through which a broad stream wound like a silver ribbon, and they rushed from one spot to another in search of new and beautiful points of view.

Suddenly Ernest stopped. 'What is that?' he asked quickly, as a sort of shrill, grating cry became audible.

The dogs pricked their ears, listened for an instant, and, on hearing the noise repeated, darted forward; but I called them back, and ordered them to remain beside me, as I wished to find out the whereabouts of the animal myself. Peering behind a projecting rock, I saw the object of my search sniffing about in evident unconsciousness of our proximity.

'Ha! An ant-eater,' I exclaimed. 'Now, boys, for a sharp fight. We are not going to have it all our own way this time, I can tell you.'

'What is an ant-eater?' asked Jack, as he gazed wonderingly at the animal. 'I never heard of one before.'

'It is, as you see, a beast of considerable size,' I replied, 'and of a greyish-brown colour. Its name is derived from its favourite article of diet. It makes sad havoc among the ant-hills, and the little insects have serious cause to dread its approach. With its long snout or front paws it scratches away the clay that covers the nest, and then demolishes its industrious occupants.'

As I spoke, Topsy and Bill rushed off, unheeding my former command, and the next moment war was declared, and hostilities commenced. I watched the contest for a few minutes, unable to decide which party was likely to be victorious; but as soon as I perceived that the sharp claws of the ant-eater were very effective weapons, I put an end to the combat by lodging the contents of my gun in the creature's head. As I believed its flesh to be most unappetizing and hardly fit for human food, I handed it over to the dogs – first taking care to cut off the tail, which Jack begged for a trophy, and which he stuck proudly in his belt.

The sun had sunk behind the western hills, and a decided chilliness had succeeded the intense heat of the afternoon, ere we recrossed the sandy waste, and deposited our baggage in front of the hut at Prospect Farm. The occurrences of the day had to be minutely detailed for Franz's benefit, for he questioned and cross-examined us about this, that, and the other thing until at last we became quite perplexed, and his mother was obliged to threaten him with corporal punishment ere he would desist.

Next morning preparations for departure were again commenced; but this time they were on a larger scale, for two – my wife and Franz – were to be added to our number, and our absence was to be of a few days' duration.

Again the desert was traversed, and soon our attention was being diverted by various objects of interest. Once, as we stopped to examine a tree of extraordinary dimensions and most peculiar foliage, Ernest moved forward, and looked into the distance in evident astonishment.

'What in the world do I see down in the valley?' he said. 'It seems as if two horsemen were moving along slowly, and a third following them at full gallop. All three are coming towards us. Can they possibly be mounted savages?'

'I don't think that is likely; but as we cannot get a good view from here, let us climb this eminence; we shall see better and feel safer,' I answered.

As soon as we had reached the tip, I produced the little telescope that was my constant companion, and by its help discovered, not mounted savages, nor anything like them, but three ostriches, which were nearing us with stately strides. When I announced this to the boys they were greatly excited.

'Oh! What a grand chase we shall have!' exclaimed Fritz. 'Do try and take one of them alive.'

'I shall certainly make the effort, but it will probably be attended with poor success, for these birds run with exceeding swiftness, as you will guess on seeing the length of their legs. Before they come nearer to us, you had better tie up the dogs, for if once they are startled and make off, it will be impossible to come up with them. Our only chance is to advance very cautiously, and take one unawares if we can.'

While the boys were attending to my suggestion regarding the dogs, the birds came nearer and nearer, sporting playfully with each other. They were five in number, and none of them was less than eight feet high. Four of them were females, and the fifth was a male. The latter could be easily distinguished by the white feathers that adorned his wings and tail, and to him we at once took a wonderful fancy.

'I think unless we creep closer to them there is no proba-bility of them being caught, for, although it is plain they have not yet perceived us, something seems to be keeping them aloof from us,' suggested Ernest.

'Indeed it would be much better,' added Jack earnestly. 'I am sure, no matter how fast they run, that I could keep up with them for a little while at any rate. But even if I could not, we might catch one, for I have read that when an ostrich sees any one in pursuit it hides its head, and then believes that it is entirely concealed.'

'There is more of romance than reality in that story, I can assure you,' I said. 'Stupidity is by no means a characteristic of this great bird. Generally when danger is at hand it is aware of it, and seeks safety in flight. Should its pursuer follow closely, it defends itself ably by throwing up stones and sand with its feet while running. As the ostrich can go faster than a horse can gallop, it would be utterly vain for us to attempt to catch it except by stratagem, as I said before.'

At this moment, the dogs, which were tied loosely to the stump of a tree, began to get impatient with their confine-ment, and gave expression to their feelings by an angry howl.

The ostriches glanced round in alarm, and as soon as they saw us scampered off with incredible speed, their outspread wings giving them the appearance of ships sailing on a sea of sand. So ended our ostrich hunt.

As we were passing through a verdant valley, which con-

trasted agreeably with the arid plains we had crossed, darkness overtook us – darkness so intense that we knew it would
be useless to attempt to proceed, though we would gladly
have passed the night in a more open locality. We groped
about as well as we could until we had collected a large
quantity of inflammable material, with which I intended to
keep a protecting circle of flame round us the whole night.
Then we stretched ourselves on the soft grass, and had no
sooner done so than the mantle of sleep enveloped us. All at
once I was awakened by a low whine, succeeded by an angry
bark, and I rose to search for the cause of Bill's annoyance.
For some minutes I could neither hear nor see anything; then
a deep growl reached my ear. Guided by the sound, I looked
beyond the fiery ring, and saw two bears marching up
and down, and appearing to consider how they could
satisfy their hunger without damaging their coats. As no
opening was visible, the larger of the two was seized with
a sudden resolve to make one for himself, and with that
object in view laid one of his forepaws on the glowing
embers; but he withdrew it instantaneously, uttering a howl
of agony.

Meanwhile I had loaded my gun, and as the brute stood
facing me, holding his scorched paw in the air as if to cool it, I
fired. Fritz, who had set himself bravely to do battle with the
second bear, fired at the same. Our first shots, though they
wounded the bears, were, unfortunately not mortal, and I
hesitated to fire again lest I should injure the dogs, who were

dragging the animals hither and thither, at the risk of their lives, with the greatest bravery.

One of them, however, could not bite, for I had with my shot broken his under jaw, and Fritz had wounded the other in the forepaw; they had, therefore, lost some of their natural strength, but not their courage. Indeed, the pain and the attacks of the dogs rendered them furious, and the struggles to defend themselves, added to their loud growls and the yelping of the dogs, rendered the scene truly fearful. The bears, sometimes erect, sometimes on all fours, fought bravely, and as I could see that the dogs were wounded and bleeding, I expected every moment to see one or two lie dead on the battlefield.

At the same time the bears appeared to grow weaker, and I therefore determined to approach nearer, and watch my opportunity to fire when close upon them. Making a sign to Fritz to follow, I went forward cautiously, and choosing a moment when the creatures were too much occupied with the dogs to notice us, I shot one of them through the head, while the ball fired by Fritz passed through the heart of the other.

'God be praised,' I murmured devoutly, as our two dangerous foes fell to the earth with a groan. 'It was fortunate that our second shots took such good effect, for had we only wounded the bears, our situation would have been a most critical one. This is a specimen of the silver bear met with by Captain Clarke on the north-west coast of America. Its fur, as

you see, is very beautiful, and may be used for many purposes.'

'If you wish to preserve it, had you not better remove the carcasses to within the circle?' asked Fritz. 'If we leave them here all night they will likely be attacked.'

'Oh, what is the use of taking the trouble to drag them away?' said Jack. 'Some one of us can keep awake, and give the alarm if we see any cause.'

'Our keeping awake would not avail much, considering the darkness,' remarked Fritz. 'Don't you know that it was only the light of the fire that enabled us to perceive the bears. As soon as the bright blaze declines, we shall be as badly off as before.'

When the boys had settled the question amongst themselves, I requested their aid in lifting the huge animals. Each measured more than eight feet in length. Their weight was very considerable, and it was not without difficulty that we got them transferred to a place of safety.

Next morning we got up – not without a struggle, which, after the fatigue of the previous day, was very excusable – and after having removed the skins from the bears, again set out. As we journeyed along, the first object of interest that we perceived was a herd of stags emerging from the shade of an extensive grove. The sight of us startled the timid animals, and several of them dashed rapidly across the meadow. Jack levelled his fowling-piece with the intention of bringing down one of the remaining ones, but just as he was about to do so, I whispered quickly, 'Stop! There is a splendid lynx. Keep as quiet as you can, and perhaps we may be able to take it. Do you see it crawling along from branch to branch, and ever with its eyes fixed on the stags?'

Jack lowered his gun, and lay down on the grass to watch the wily animal as it bounded from tree to tree, until it stood just above the spot where the herd must pass. As the last stag went by it sprang on its back, and fastened its cruel teeth in its neck. The beautiful creature sank gasping to the earth, while its scared companions fled through the valley.

'Ought we not now to attack the murderer?' asked Jack.

'Yes. You and Fritz can creep quietly along the ground, and fire when you think you are within range,' I replied.

The two huntsmen approached noiselessly, and were unperceived by the lynx, which had eyes for nothing but its prey. Two shots were fired, and their effect was instantaneous. The wounded animal leaped into the air, and then fell quivering beside its victim.

Towards evening that day, while we were partaking of supper, we were disturbed by hearing a noise like the rushing of wind; yet no leaf stirred, not the faintest ripple ruffled the surface of the lake that slumbered at our feet. Louder and louder grew the sound, and we sat gazing at each other in speechless wonder. At last the phenomenon was explained by the appearance of a flock of antelopes, which galloped towards us, apparently unaware of our presence. When they had arrived within a few hundred feet of us their speed lessened; by degrees they stopped altogether, and began to browse quietly. This seemed the moment for our attack. Cautiously and rapidly we advanced, but in spite of our care some sound warned the animals of danger; they bounded off gracefully, tossing their heads and pricking up their ears, and in a few minutes they disappeared completely from view.

On the following day we set off back for home, as the rainy season was too close to allow us to remain absent any longer.

CHAPTER XV

FARMING AND FISHING

O UR THIRD winter passed uneventfully. Again we all found plenty to occupy us in the grotto, although often we looked out at the torrential rain and longed for it to cease. One day my wife recalled to my memory a promise that I had made some time previously, and asked me when I intended turning my hand to the manufacture of porcelain.

'You know,' she said, 'you have a large bagful of the proper sort of clay, and I have been looking forward so hopefully to possessing a pretty dinner service, that I shall feel greatly disappointed if you do not at least try to provide me with one.'

'I shall make the attempt with all my heart,' said I; 'but I do not feel very hopeful regarding the result. I fear your plates will be anything but symmetrical; but let us suppose there is no such word as "fail", and try to win fresh laurels on the field of pottery.'

Out of an old cannon wheel I constructed a lathe, and on this I formed plates, saucers, cups, and vessels of various kinds. In order to beautify the new ware, I broke up a number of coloured beads and other glass ornaments and mixed them with the clay paste. The effect was by no means

bad. By dint of perseverance we made a quantity of crockery which my wife pronounced to be above criticism. The boys did not judge my products so leniently. Jack remarked of my saucers that they only required ribs to be fine umbrellas, and my intended coffee-cups were said to bear a stronger resemblance to wash-tubs than anything else. This occupation was succeeded by many others of minor importance, and numerous useful and ornamental additions were made to our furniture.

The winter over, our first job was to make an expedition to Falcon's Nest, to see how it had stood up to the storms. Much to our surprise and satisfaction, we found that the past rains had done so little damage to the Nest that a few hours' work would restore it to its former state. As evening fell we gathered under the sheltering roof of our aerial abode, and chatted about the work which the morrow had in store for us. Suddenly we heard a loud mocking laugh, and a thrill of horror ran through us at the hateful sound.

'What in the world can that be?' asked my wife.

While she spoke, another peal of laughter, louder and more fiendish than the former, rang out on the night air, and Franz set up a cry of alarm.

'Hush!' I said. 'It is only a four-footed foe that we have to deal with, though one of the most detestable creatures that infest the earth. It is a hyena, and has likely been attracted hither by the smell of the stag's flesh. A dead animal has more attraction for it than a living one, and it has often been known to scratch open the graves of men and feast on their contents. Let us have a shot at the hateful beast.'

My wife besought me not to rush heedlessly into danger, but when I told her that the hyena is celebrated for its cowardice, and would run any distance rather than turn and face its pursuer, her fears were quieted, and she allowed the three eldest boys to descend with me. For some minutes we could distinguish nothing; but as our eyes became accustomed to the darkness, we perceived at a little distance from the tree two forms which we presumed to be those of the animals of which we were in search. A low bay from the dogs that we kept in the background seemed to alarm the cowardly creatures. They sprang suddenly aside, but in fleeing from one enemy they ran to meet another. Their movements brought them in close proximity to us, so, raising our guns, Fritz and I fired. The two beasts rolled over on the grass without a struggle.

For a week after this we remained at Falcon's Nest in the enjoyment of comparative idleness, but at the end of that

time we began to long for active employment, and set out for
our corn-field in order to see in what condition the crop was.

To our surprise we found that the land which had been
tilled only three or four months before was covered with an
abundant growth of ripe corn, and from this fact we drew the
gratifying conclusion that henceforth we should be able to
reckon on two harvests every year. The potatoes and cassava roots were also fit to be gathered in, and the time was at
hand when the herring shoal, with its train of gluttonous
white fish, would reach the coast. So from having nothing to
occupy us, we were suddenly so overwhelmed with work that
we hardly knew what to do first. Thinking that the vegetables would derive little injury from remaining a week or
two longer in the soil, we decided to look after the cereal
harvest; but in order to hasten the ingathering as much as
possible, I thought it advisable to adopt the old Italian plan

of reaping. Though not so economical as other methods, it is much more expeditious, and it was time that we were anxious to save in the present case. Without delay, therefore, we cleared away a large space in a little sheltered vale close to the field, and there we intended to thresh the grain in the ancient manner – that is, to have it trodden out by oxen. As soon as this was done we betook ourselves to the field and commenced operations. Our mode of reaping was to lay hold of as many ears as we could with the left hand and cut them off with the right, taking away as little straw as possible, and throwing the decapitated ears into a basket.

Before evening the field was reaped and the corn carried to the valley to be threshed. This was rare occupation for the boys, who mounted on their steeds and trod out the grain in a couple of hours. As soon as the chaff was separated from the grain we stored it in our granary in the grotto, and it afforded us much satisfaction to perceive that never before had we had such an abundant crop.

In order to obtain a second harvest it was necessary to begin sowing again at once. In this operation we adopted the Swiss method – namely, that of changing the crop periodically. We had just reaped corn and wheat; we now sowed maize and rye.

Our work was hardly completed when the expected herring shoal made its appearance in the bay and occupied our attention exclusively. We secured several barrelfuls of the delicate fish, and having salted them, laid them aside for

future use. While we were so engaged, we noticed now and
again large animals appearing above the water for a minute
or two, and then diving below the surface. At first we
thought they might be young whales, but this opinion careful observation proved to be incorrect.

One day Ernest begged me to allow him to paddle out into
the bay to gratify his curiosity respecting the character of
our visitors. Having gained my permission, he embarked in
our boat (in which he had already placed the harpoon and
gun), and shot over the water like an arrow towards the part
where several of the strange animals were sporting. On
approaching quite close to them he recognized them to be
walruses, and he conceived the desire to take one of them
home for the gratification of his brothers. But before he was
able to carry out his intention, the walruses, as if aware of his
murderous inclination, dived below the water and did not
reappear until they had removed to a safe distance from him.
On his return, his brothers were so excited by his description
of the strange creatures, with their ox-shaped heads and long
tusks, that I was obliged to promise to engage in their
pursuit, should they favour us with another visit.

The reappearance of the walruses next morning was the
signal for a joyful shout from the children, and also for
the preparation of the pinnace. Lest any accident should
happen, I took care to put a lot of bladders and corkwood
on board. As soon as these and a necessary supply of provisions were stowed away, we set out, followed by the anxious

eyes of my wife, who remained with Franz on land.

We were sailing towards a group of about thirty seahorses. Not wishing to rush into the midst of such a company, I resigned my intention of using the harpoon, and decided on trying the effect of my gun instead. Loading it, and telling Fritz to do the same with his, we fired. Simultaneously with the double report was heard a loud splash, as the animals disappeared below the water. On one alone did our shots seem to have taken effect, and it I soon dragged on board amid the hurrahs of the onlookers. Our attack seemed to have frightened the walruses most effectually, for, though we floated about the place for an hour, we could perceive no further trace of them.

When we were about to turn the vessel homewards, Jack, who was leaning over the stern gazing out to sea, called: 'Look! Look! Father, that must be a giant seahorse, for it is far larger than any of those that we saw a little while ago. Do try to get it. It is worth half a dozen of the others.'

'I shall certainly do my best, but if failure rewards me, you must not be disappointed,' I replied. Then seizing the harpoon, I threw it, and at the same moment two balls which Ernest and Fritz had discharged from their guns whistled through the air, and lodged in the animal's side. For some time it struggled violently; but the determined hold which we kept on the rope of the harpoon that had been fastened in its back prevented its escape. Little by little its struggles became weaker, until we were able to draw it after us.

'It is not a walrus, Jack,' I said, 'but a sea lion, or ursine seal. These creatures are very common in the waters round Cape Horn and in the neighbourhood of those islands that lie north of Chile. Its skin will be useful to us for covering boxes and for other similar purposes.'

Landing at a small island in the bay, we deprived the sea lion of its hide, and the walrus of its tusks and fat, and then got on board the pinnace again and set sail for home. During the afternoon the clouds had been growing gradually more threatening, and there were many indications of a change of weather. Before we had completed the half of our journey, one of those hurricanes that are of such frequent occurrence in tropical countries burst upon us. Rain fell in torrents from the overcharged clouds; the wind howled and whistled as if revelling in its power, and the waves rolled mountains high, now lifting our slight bark on their foam-crested tops, now plunging it beneath an avalanche of water. One moment deep abysses yawned below and threatened to engulf us; the next saw us raised to a dizzy height on a gigantic billow. Louder pealed the thunder overhead, more vivid grew the lightning flashes, and my hope of weathering the storm became each instant fainter.

As it was useless to think of attempting to land, I turned my vessel out to sea, and thus avoided the rocks and sands, on which, had I ventured inland, we should certainly have been dashed by the waves. For more than two hours the tempest raged with unabated fury. Then the sea became

calmer, the winds fell, and the black clouds cleared away, showing the smiling sky beyond. The squall subsided as suddenly as it had arisen, and again we directed our course landward.

On landing we were welcomed by my wife and Franz, who were overjoyed at our safe return. After a hearty supper, we retired to rest.

CHAPTER XVI

FRITZ AND JACK EXPLORE

SEVERAL TIMES of late the boys had urged me to allow them to set out alone on an expedition of a few days' duration. They were anxious to visit Prospect Hill and Forest Farm, and to push their explorations to the right and left of this route, and they knew I would not willingly absent myself for a lengthened period from my wife and Franz. When my permission was first sought, my fears lest they should expose themselves to danger made me refuse to grant it, but during the last few weeks they had behaved so wisely in several trying circumstances that I resolved to gratify them. Accordingly I said one morning, 'If you still wish to set out on the voyage of discovery of which you have so often spoken, I will no longer withhold my consent. The weather is favourable, and there is little at present to occupy you about home.'

A loud 'huzzah' testified the delight which my remarks afforded, and the boys at once commenced their preparations. The filling of their game-bags with provisions occupied them a considerable time, as they experienced some difficulty in selecting what each liked, and what would keep fresh for several days. At last I said, 'I think if you would take some pemmican with you, you would find it very much to your taste. It is prepared from bear's and deer's flesh pounded into a sort of paste, and is greatly esteemed by Canadian fur-dealers during their long excursions into the interior of the country.' This seemed to be the very thing that was wanted, and my wife at once began to beat the meat and make it up into little balls, so that it could be easily carried. While she was thus occupied, the boys busied themselves plaiting rod baskets, mending our partly-worn sacks, and making new bird-snares. The sledge was got ready, and on it were piled bows and arrows, guns, ammunition, victuals and various other things which the travellers considered they might require before their return. A cage containing a few of our European pigeons was placed on the top of the load. I was at a loss to understand why they wished to have these useless companions, but as they evidently desired to be mysterious on the subject, I did not press them to tell.

The morning of departure at length arrived, and at an early hour there was a general movement in our camp. Much to our surprise, Ernest, at the last moment, expressed a desire to stay at home, so Fritz and Jack were left to brave the dangers of the journey alone. The last word of advice was given, the last good-bye was said, and amid shouts of farewell and encouragement the two young explorers disappeared from our view – but not before their mother had extracted a promise from them to return on the evening of the third day.

The first day of their absence was spent by Ernest and myself in erecting a machine for crushing rice and compressing the sugar-cane. The task was one of considerable difficulty, but in the end the work was finished.

After supper we gathered on the balcony to enjoy the cool air of the evening, and to listen to the sweet concert with which our feathered neighbours had agreed to delight us.

'I wish I had some means of knowing how Fritz and Jack are engaged at present,' I said. 'I have had neither peace nor rest since they left, and I am continually imagining them in some dangerous predicament.' As I spoke, one of the pigeons flew past me and entered the cote in the hollow of the tree. 'I wonder what unusual sport was going on today. The pigeons are generally shut in an hour or two before this time,' I said, turning to Ernest, but he had disappeared.

In a few minutes he returned, and coming up to me smilingly, asked, 'What would you give for news of the wanderers? How will you reward the postman if he brings you a letter from them?'

I gazed at him in astonishment, and wondered what he meant by such apparently foolish questions. 'Why! How can you ask anything so silly? There is no postman within hundreds of miles of us, unfortunately, and how could I reward one?'

For answer he held towards me a piece of paper, on the back of which was written: 'Despatch from the explorers, Fritz and Jack, to His Majesty the King of New Switzerland.'

On unfolding the sheet, I read:

May it please your Majesty.

'The explorers whom your Majesty was graciously pleased to appoint to conduct the expedition to North Island report that as yet all has gone well with them. They beg humbly to return their grateful thanks to your Majesty for the confidence reposed in them. It is expected that verbal information regarding the movements of your Majesty's servants will be given at Fortress Castle two days hence.

(Signed) FRITZ and JACK,

Explorers of North Island.

When I had finished the perusal of the note, Franz clapped his hands gleefully and said, 'Now, father, you are surely happy since you know that no evil has befallen my brothers. They seem to have met with no adventures, or else they were so much afraid of being disrespectful to "your Majesty", that they would not dare to relate them.'

'But, my dear boy, this is Ernest's work, you know. How in the world could a letter reach us from the other side of the island?'

At this Ernest laughed heartily, and hastened to assure me that the despatch had really been sent by the absent ones. The ingenious boys had fastened it under the wing of the pigeon, and when the bird was set free, instinct had guided it back to its abode. Next day a second feathered messenger arrived, and delivered a letter which was much more satisfactory than the first. It ran as follows:

DEAR FATHER,

We are achieving glorious victories over the four-footed inhabitants of the island! Jack has already slaughtered a large buffalo, the skin of which he intends presenting to mother for a mantle, and the horns to you for drinking vessels. He says truly that the offerings are neither handsome nor useful, but he has nothing else. We had a bit of rare fun with a hyena today, but its laughter was turned to tears before we had done with it. It is a pity Ernest is not with us. Love to mother and all, from

FRITZ and JACK.

From time to time during the succeeding days similar missives to this reached us, so we were kept informed of the well-being of the boys. On the evening of the third day the blowing of Jack's old trumpet announced the return of the wanderers, and we set out to meet them. As soon as the cart was unloaded and the animals housed and fed, we all re-entered our dwelling, and I begged the boys to give us a full account of their excursion.

'Before leaving home,' began Fritz, 'we had determined to pursue a different route altogether to those we had already traversed, so instead of advancing as usual towards the source of Jackal River, we went in the very opposite direction. We had not gone far when we arrived at a large wood, in the very centre of which was a little meadow covered with soft fresh grass. It looked so sweet and tender that we dismounted in order that our steeds might graze for a few minutes. We had scarcely done so when a whole herd of buffaloes dashed across the field, tossing their manes and snorting loudly, as if annoyed by something.

'"What a pity," said Jack, lifting his gun to see that it was loaded, "that we had not time to fire. I should like to be avenged on those brutes for the fright one of the tribe once gave me."

'As he spoke, a black head appeared from between the trees on our left, and three animals that had straggled behind their companions walked leisurely along, seemingly unaware of our presence.

'"Now is your time," I whispered. "Keep your hand steady and fire."

'Immediately a loud report was heard. Two of the buffaloes galloped off in wild alarm; the third fell dead on the spot. We lost no time in transferring the carcass to the cart, intending to skin it when we arrived at some place where there would be less danger of being disturbed by beasts of prey.

'After marching almost the whole afternoon under the heat of a broiling sun, we fell into a road which we recognized to be one leading to Forest Farm. Though this was by no means the goal we had in view when we left home, we were nevertheless not sorry to arrive at a spot on which even the most fragile hut had been erected; for night was coming on, and we did not relish the idea of passing it under the stars.

'As we trudged along contentedly, conversing about adventures past and future, Jack paused suddenly and said: "Listen! I heard such a funny noise just this minute. It seemed as if some one was shaking peas in a tin pan."

' "Your vivid imagination is playing you a trick again," I said, laughing at his description of the sound. "How could one get peas in this uncivilized corner of the world; and if they were to be had, how could even such a primitive utensil as a tin pan be obtained?"

'Just as I finished speaking the rattle again became audible, and from the description that he had given us of the noise made by a rattlesnake, I guessed one of them was at hand. I was not mistaken. From the hollow trunk of a decayed tree on our right appeared the head of a snake. Seeing that not a minute was to be lost, I raised my gun and fired. Jack did the same, and one of the balls pierced the neck of the reptile. In order to assure myself that it was really lifeless, I crept near to where it lay quite motionless, and lodged a bullet in its head; but no movement took place, and I saw with intense thankfulness that the dangerous reptile was dead. As soon as we had arrived at Forest Farm, and satisfied our appetites with a portion of the pemmican and some of the other good things that mother prepared for us, we wrote our first despatch and confided it to the care of the pigeon, which I am glad to see fulfilled its trust so well. Then, laying our heads on the pillows that you insisted should form part of our cargo, we fell asleep, and slept undisturbed till morning.

'The next morning we made for a large plantation, which, you will remember, lies not far from Forest Farm. Our journey through it was tedious and wearisome, for grass and briars tripped us at every step, and sometimes a perfect network of creeping plants filled up the spaces between the trees, so that our progress was effectually barred, and we were obliged to hew a path with our axes. It was in this grove that we had the encounter with the hyena, which I mentioned in one of my despatches. We should likely have passed it by unobserved, had not its nasty laugh betrayed its presence. But as soon as I heard the sound, I determined to bag the brute, if possible. When we first perceived it, it was standing over the remains of some animal which it had slain, and appeared undecided whether or not to begin the repast. The hideous cries that it now and again uttered had the effect of terrifying our steeds greatly, and Jack was obliged to keep a tight hold on them lest they should run away. I was therefore obliged to brave the encounter single-handed. Having loaded my pistols, I stuck them in my belt, and then, taking up my gun, I advanced cautiously towards the hyena. My approach was unnoticed, except by an angry glance from its flaming eyes and a low, barking whine. It seemed too intent on the prey which it had now commenced to devour to trouble itself about me.

'While it stood quietly feasting I had a good opportunity for taking aim. I fired both barrels, and was fortunate enough to hit each time, but neither of the wounds was deadly. One of its forepaws, however, was broken, and this prevented it either from fleeing or rushing upon me. I whistled on Brown and Fawn to come to my aid, and when they had arrived at the scene of action, a bloody contest ensued between them and the infuriated, though disabled hyena. The dogs had at first quite enough to do to defend themselves, but in a short time their antagonist became weak through loss of blood, and the combat was brought to a close by its death. We then skinned the carcass, and continued our journey. Some distance farther on we came upon a beautiful valley, in the middle of which was a lake. In order to reach the edge of the water it was necessary to traverse a marsh in which grew the tallest reeds I ever saw.

As we passed through it flocks of birds rose and flew over our heads; but their appearance was so sudden, and their flight so rapid, that we thought it useless to attempt to bring any of them down. Just once Jack plucked up his courage and fired. He was rewarded by seeing a magnificent bird, which I take to be a sultan cock, falling at his feet. It had only been wounded in the wing, so he tied it up carefully and brought it to Franz, who, I have no doubt, will prize it greatly. As soon as we had admired the lake as it sparkled in the sunlight, and tried to catch some of the brilliantly-coloured winged insects that floated over its glittering surface, we retraced our steps, as the second day of our leave had almost drawn to a close. As we were about to re-enter the plantation, Jack turned round to take a last look at the gorgeous landscape that lay behind us.

' "See there," he said, clutching me so tightly by the arm that even yet I seem to feel his hold on my flesh. "What can that animal be that is sneaking after us? When I glanced back it was following us cautiously, and now that we have stopped it has done the same. What can it be?"

' "I expect it is the puma, or American lion, whose appearance and habits father described to us the other day," I replied. "It is a very cowardly beast, and would hardly dare to follow us even at a distance, had not hunger rendered it unusually brave. When it sees us looking at it, it will soon disappear."

'Even as I spoke, the animal turned and scampered off in

the opposite direction to where we stood. It was with difficulty that I could dissuade Jack from pursuing it. The little
madcap was most anxious to secure its skin as a trophy, and
it was only by pointing out to him to what danger our cattle
would be exposed did we leave them that I could prevail on
him to continue his way.

'After about an hour's march we sat down to rest and
refresh ourselves, and to allow our beasts of burden to do the
same. We had hardly unpacked the provision bag, when the
dogs began to whine and growl, and show other signs of
uneasiness.

' "I'll bet," says Jack, who was straining his eyes and
looking towards the path we had just traversed, "I'll bet the
puma is again behind us. I see something moving amongst
the long grass, and I know no other animal that would
approach with so much hesitancy."

' "Very probably it has renewed the pursuit, and trusts to
chance to being unperceived," I rejoined. "This time we shall
not allow it to escape, if possible. Let us stretch ourselves on
the ground, and pretend to be asleep, and when it has come
near enough let us fire."

'The plan was instantaneously put into execution. Even
our dumb companions seemed to understand our desire for
silence, and tried to gratify it. For some time we lay quite
still, listening intently; but nothing could be heard but the
hoarse croaking of the frogs in the swamp, and the shrill cry
of the water-fowl.

' "There is no use in staying here any longer," said Jack, at last, raising his head. "We must have been mistaken in thinking the faint-hearted beast was on our track."

'I signed to him to keep quiet, for at that moment I heard a faint rustling among the long dry grass, and took it for a sign of our enemy's approach. The next instant it sprang from its place of concealment, and alighted on the branch of a tree just in front of us. On seeing that we were awake, it mounted quickly towards the top, as if to get out of our reach, but that was not so easily accomplished. Levelling our guns, we both fired, and the puma fell a victim to its own hardihood. Its skin was then added to our other possessions, and its flesh handed over to the dogs.

'After we had despatched another letter home, we erected our tent, and lighted a fire round it before we retired. During the night our slumbers were occasionally disturbed by the howling of the jackals and other beasts of prey, but as they seemed to be at a considerable distance from us we thought it better to remain quietly under cover than to show ourselves and invite an attack. Next morning, as soon as we had breakfasted, we set out and moved forward rapidly, and arrived here without further adventure.'

'Bravo!' I exclaimed, as Fritz finished his recital. 'But you and Jack behaved most wisely and courageously, and have gained my entire confidence. I shall have no fear again in allowing you to make an excursion alone whenever you wish, as I know you will act as prudently as you would if under my eye. The account of your trip has interested us all greatly, and the evidence of your bravery which you have brought home will be highly prized. In the name of the King of New Switzerland and his loyal subjects, I tender the explorers warmest thanks for both.'

As I said this Franz waved his plumed hat in the air and shouted, 'Long live the explorers,' and a loud 'huzzah' went up from him and Ernest in testimony of their pleasure at their brothers' safe return.

Next morning we unloaded the car of its treasures, and for many days our time was taken up with stuffing rare and beautiful birds for our museum, preparing the skins of the various animals that had been shot, and cutting up and salting the flesh of a few deer that Ernest had found in full enjoyment of the pleasures of the salt lick, and had taken. As compensation for being kept working so closely, I promised my sons, as soon as our several pressing duties were performed, to take a trip to the small island that we had called Shark Island. In accordance with my promise, one beautiful morning we got ready the pinnace, and prepared to set out. The sea was so blue and unruffled, and our little vessel looked so safe and pretty, that my wife forgot her fears, and expressed a desire to accompany us. The lightness and rapidity with which the ship danced over the waves were delightful to our new passenger; her former prejudices against the sea were entirely obliterated, and ever after she was as anxious for a sail as the youngest and most daring of her family.

'What would you think,' asked Fritz, as we stood on the summit of the only hill the island could boast, and surveyed our little territory, which in the distance seemed nothing but a chain of rocks, and the almost endless waste of waters that surrounded it, 'what would you think of building a sort of fortress – or, to speak less ambitiously, a sentinel's box – here? The view on every side is much more extensive than that to be had from any other part of our dominion. If we had reason to expect an invasion of the savages, or the approach of a ship, we could easily verify our suspicions by looking out from our watch-tower.'

'The idea seems to be not a bad one,' I replied. 'In times of danger one of you could take up your abode here for a few days, and a system of signals could be established, so that the movements of each might be known to the other. What would you think, boys, of laying the foundation-stone now, as we have nothing better to do? If tomorrow be fine, we could return and finish the job.'

My proposition was unanimously agreed to, and the active young workmen commenced to gather together the materials. When the necessary things were collected, we drove four strong poles into the ground, and twisted bamboos out and in amongst them so as to form wickerwork walls. In three sides we made little openings, at a distance of about five feet from the ground, through which the sentinel could see without being seen, and in the fourth a larger opening served as a door. Inside this gigantic cage we scraped two large holes, in one of which we intended to keep a quantity of ammunition, and in the other some provisions, so that should the watchman be besieged, he might not be compelled to capitulate through hunger. Both these cavities were covered with a large flat stone, over which a few inches of earth was spread so as to conceal them effectually. The boys carried on the work with such zeal and strength that, greatly to my astonishment, it was completed before nightfall, and all that remained to be done on the occasion of our next visit was to place a cannon in the sentry-box by which signals could be given to us, and death dealt to unwelcome invaders.

Our return journey was as pleasant and uneventful as that to the island had been, and we disembarked at Deliverance Bay, delighted with our excursion. As soon as we had landed, Fritz and Jack set off towards the grotto at full speed, with the laudable intention of having the fire kindled and everything in working order before their mother was ready to see about preparing supper. Their design, however, was frustrated, and their race interrupted, by the sight of what they supposed to be several human beings marching leisurely up and down in front of the cave. They ran back to us, and gasped rather than said, 'Don't go any farther. There are horrible creatures beyond; they are armed with long sticks, and will be sure to attack us if we appear.'

'Are they savages?' I asked. 'If so, I have nothing to fear, for they proved themselves anything but invincible in our former encounters.'

'Oh, no,' replied Jack; 'they are far more terrible-looking

than savages. Their bodies are covered with long dark hair, and their arms seem half as long again as they ought to be. When we first saw them, they were walking round and round in a circle, and chatting loudly.'

'I must venture nearer these phenomena,' I said. 'Your description has roused my curiosity, but has suggested to my mind no animal that I ever saw or heard of. Who wants to obtain a closer view of the hairy men, or whatever they may be?'

My wife and Franz shuddered at the very thought of the unseen monsters, and Fritz and Jack considered they had seen as much of them as was desirable. So Ernest and I marched on alone. When we were yet at some distance from our dwelling, the chattering of which Jack had told us was distinctly audible; but it was not till we were quite close to it that we perceived, sitting in the shade of a projecting rock, the beings who were giving utterance to the sounds. It was a group of orang-outangs, who appeared to be engaged in some game, and so intent were they on their amusement that for a good while we stood watching them unobserved. At last they turned round and seeing us, scampered into the wood, screaming with terror.

'I don't wonder that your brothers mistook these curious creatures for human beings,' I said to Ernest, 'for – unflattering though the statement be – they bear so close a resemblance to our race that they are often called "wild men of the woods".'

'The likeness is indeed very striking,' responded Ernest,

'and affords some ground for the theory that apes are a species of the genus man. But as the thought of being akin to these ugly brutes is anything but pleasant, I have no desire to entertain it.'

We now shouted to those behind to come on, as all danger was removed; and soon we were gathered once more in our comfortable sitting-room, doing justice to the tempting food that my wife placed before us. Part of it was a stew made from a pair of the rabbits which Fritz had shot while on his expedition with Jack. It was so excellent that we conceived the desire of securing a large number of the little animals, and decided to proceed on the following day to the hill east of Jackal River, where they were to be found in great numbers.

CHAPTER XVII

PEARL FISHING

THE NEXT morning we again barricaded the door and window, harnessed the cow, whistled on the dogs, and set off in the expectation of a good day's sport. As the heat was intense, our journey occupied us longer than we anticipated, for we frequently found it necessary to sit down and rest under the agreeable shade of some overhanging tree or rock. It was almost midday when we arrived at the 'Rabbit Warren', as the boys called the spot we were about to visit. When we were about a few hundred paces from the hill, we could see a countless host of the nimble creatures trotting up and down; but as we drew near they vanished in an instant, without leaving a trace behind them.

'They can't have been rabbits at all,' said Franz, who knew nothing of the animals or their habits. 'No earthly things could have disappeared with the rapidity that those did. One moment they were there, and next – whiff! And they were off just as if they had shot through the ground.'

'Which is exactly what they did,' I interrupted. 'Rabbits, unlike other animals with which you are well acquainted, live in holes that they burrow in the soil, and those which we saw this moment have only taken refuge in their underground homes till we go past.'

'But if they don't come out, how are we to get at them? We could not crawl in after them and pull them out by the tails.'

'If you attempted that, you would find you had not much to hold by,' I said, laughing. 'No, we shall not intrude into their domiciles, but I shall lay the traps that you saw me making last night in front of them, and whenever they come out they will walk unsuspiciously into them. If we had a ferret we might have a few hours' good sport, for the little animal would poke its way, in spite of all obstacles, to the spot where the rabbits lie hidden, and would drive them out.'

We then set all the traps that I had brought with me and withdrew, so that the timid animals might pluck up courage and emerge from their dens.

'What is that?' exclaimed Jack, pointing towards a high rock, which stood like a monument in the midst of a little plantation.

'Why, what could it be but a rock?' I asked.

'Oh! I don't mean that,' he rejoined, hurriedly. 'But a beast that is standing close to it, and gazing steadfastly at something in the distance. It is about the size of a badger, and of a light brown colour. Don't you see it? Look! It moves forward cautiously, and seems about to spring.'

'Ah, yes! There it is now! I think it is a curious animal commonly called the glutton, on account of its ravenous appetite and its carelessness regarding the quality of its food. Hens, rabbits, deer, in short everything is demolished by it.

It has even been known to attack horses and reindeer, and shepherds in the north of Europe and America could tell you long stories of its raids amongst their flocks.'

While we were conversing in whispers regarding the animal, it mounted on a little jutting ledge of the rock, and sprang on some unsuspecting and unoffending creature that was resting quietly below. A sharp cry of pain and fright succeeded; but a shot from Ernest put an end to the murderous assault, and the glutton was destined to fill a vacant corner in our museum. We now returned to the 'Rabbit Warren', and found that our traps were almost all occupied. By setting them for a few times we supplied ourselves with a large number of the animals.

While we were sitting over our dinner my wife proposed that, instead of returning home that night, as we intended when we set out, we should extend our journey and penetrate a little farther into this part of the island, which was unknown ground to us. I need hardly say that her suggestion was heartily seconded by the boys, and as I had no reason for desiring to go against it, we gathered our traps, took up our pilgrims' staves again, and trudged on. After having proceeded for some distance along a road entirely new to us, we arrived at a wide valley which particularly claimed our attention. An endless multitude of flowering plants clothed it with brilliant colours, and the vegetation was of tropical luxuriance. High cliffs rose up majestically and seemed to lose themselves in the clouds; little rivers wound their way

through brake and bramble, and, rippling downwards, emp-
tied themselves into the sea. Along their banks grew graceful
willows, whose hanging branches kissed the water, and on
whose tops perched countless birds, the plumage of which
almost dazzled one with its brilliancy. Animals of all descriptions roved about in savage tranquillity. Here an enormous
rhinoceros stood devouring the thorny leaves of the cactus;
there a herd of elephants marched forward slowly and un-
gracefully, as if wearied with the weight of their colossal
bodies; farther on a troop of monkeys jabbered and chattered
as they swung themselves on the lofty trees, and tried to
rival each other in agility.

Meanwhile the boys prowled around with their guns, and
an occasional shot told us that their search after game was
not fruitless. All at once we heard Jack's voice calling:

'Father! Mother! Where are you?'

'Here,' I answered, being unable to describe the locality
better, and hoping the sound of my voice would guide him to
us. 'What is wrong? Has another lobster caught you by the
leg? Or have you mistaken a withered branch for a rattlesnake, and are you fleeing from the dangerous reptile?'

'Ah, father!' he rejoined complainingly, 'you are always
making fun of me.'

Then he appeared, carrying in his hand one of the most
beautiful birds I had ever seen – a bird of paradise.

Its chief beauty consisted in a tail more than two feet in
length, the feathers of which glowed with the most beautiful

shades of green, gold, and brown, terminating in a spot of velvety blackness.

'Why are birds of this kind called birds of paradise?' asked Jack. 'Are they believed to have been special favourites with Adam and Eve when they were luxuriating in the garden long ago, and is no earthly spot considered to be a worthy home for them?'

'An idea something like that prevailed amongst the ancients, and curious traditions were handed down from generation to generation regarding them. One assertion was that they had no feet.'

'No feet!' interposed Jack in astonishment. 'How in the world were they supposed to get on without them?'

'The theory was that they never alighted on the earth till the moment of death, but flew on in endless motion – even sleeping and eating on the wing.'

'What an absurdity! How could sensible people believe such a thing?'

'It is astonishing what a capacity even sensible people have for swallowing the wonderful, as is proved by the fact that up till the close of the seventeenth century this absurdity, as you rightly term it, was confidently accredited. It was not till science came and dispersed the clouds of superstition which hung around this beautiful bird that it was discovered to resemble others of the feathered genus, and to be peculiarly remarkable only on account of its gorgeous plumage.'

When the other boys saw the treasure that had been procured for the museum they were delighted. But it seemed to me that a little jealousy mingled with their pleasure, and the game which they had bagged, and which a few moments before had been a source of pride and congratulation, was now regarded with evident disfavour.

On we marched steadily till near the evening, when we pitched our tent on a grassy eminence near the mouth of a wide river. While my sons busied themselves in collecting fuel for a fire, and my wife unpacked the provision bag with a view to satisfying our hunger, I unharnessed the beasts and led them down to the river to drink. What was my surprise to see that, instead of hastening to refresh themselves with a cooling draught after the exertions of the day, they refused to go within a couple of yards of the bank, and stood looking uneasily towards the other side. In vain I urged them on. They obstinately refused to move a step. I was at a loss to explain their conduct, for I could see nothing among the trees and thick shrubbery calculated to alarm them. But thinking instinct had made them aware of the presence of some foe, I was about to return to the tent for my gun when a shot was fired, evidently a good distance up the river, and a troop of splendid wild horses dashed into the water, tossing their manes and tails wildly, and snorting and neighing as if the victims of bewildering terror. However, when intending to flee from danger they rushed headlong into it; for Fritz, the report of whose gun had terrified them, was on the opposite side of the river to that which they had just quitted, he being on the same bank with me, but farther up.

I stood and watched the horses as they swam boldly towards the shore, and thought of some means of capturing one of them. All at once new fear seemed to seize them. They plunged madly about, now turning towards one bank, now towards the other, and dashed against each other as if they hardly knew what they were doing, or where they ought to go. Advancing to the edge of the water I saw a couple of sea monsters, resembling serpents both in size and form, striving to annoy the four-footed intruders on their domain in every way in their power. But ere long they seemed to grow wearied of the sport and swam to the shore, where they stretched themselves half-in half-out of the water, leaving the horses to regain the other side, which they did in a twinkling. Unfastening the axe that I always carried attached to my side by a leather strap, I struck one of the exhausted reptiles a blow on the head and killed it. It was an electric eel, or cramp-fish, similar to those that are found so commonly in the American lakes. When I discovered this I called on Fritz to come for it, as I knew it would be an attractive addition to our curiosities.

We passed the night without having our rest disturbed by any visitant, and the next morning commenced our return journey. But though our march was uninterrupted, it was evening before we arrived at the Fortress. The only thing of any consequence which I discovered on the way was a plant called euphorbia, or wolf's milk, that grew in abundance among the rocks, and whose juice is one of the most subtle poisons in the world. It is much used by the inhabitants of the Cape of Good Hope for poisoning brooks of which wild beasts are accustomed to drink. By this means the animals are killed and their rich furs procured without any trouble. I thought the euphorbia would enable me to decrease the number of monkeys that infested the island, and did so much damage to our possessions. I also knew it would be useful in preparing the skins of birds and other animals, for it preserves them effectually from corruption, and keeps out all insects.

One day, some weeks after this excursion, Ernest and Jack, who in the meantime had taken many trips alone, begged me to accompany them on a little sea voyage which they were desirous of making in the pinnace. As I was almost as anxious for a sail as they were, I accepted the invitation cordially. Fritz, Franz, and my wife were unfortunately unable to join the party, for the former had hurt his arm badly with a hatchet, Franz was laid up with a severe cold, and their mother felt obliged to remain and tend the invalids. Not a cloud was visible on the blue expanse overhead; not even a ripple disturbed the mirror-like surface of the water as we embarked, after having taken a fond leave of those who were reluctantly remaining behind.

Owing to the calmness of the weather we resolved to attempt to land on a rocky point of our territory, just opposite Whale Island, which we had several times tried to gain but without success, for when the sea was at all disturbed, it was impossible to approach without the risk of being stranded on the rocks. Nearer and nearer we came to the coast, and clearer and shallower grew the water, until at last not the smallest pebble lying at the bottom was hidden from our view. The boys gazed into the glassy depths delightedly, now admiring some exquisite shell lying in a bed of bright-coloured sea-weed, again a strange fish that darted past them, fleeing from a hungry pursuer.

Suddenly Jack said, 'This must be a regular bed of oysters, father.'

'These seem very much larger and finer than any I have ever seen,' I said, as I looked over the side of the pinnace.

Taking the harpoon, Jack cut the filaments which bound the oysters to the rocks, and brought up several to the surface. I tried to open one of the oysters with a large knife, and in doing so I felt the blade pressing against some hard substance which I thrust aside. What was my astonishment, on separating the shells, to find a pearl of wonderful beauty inside.

'Hurrah!' shouted Ernest, as I held it out for his inspection. 'That is a discovery of no mean value! Why, father, if these are all pearl oysters our riches are inestimable. If we could only turn them into money we might buy up all the millionaires of whom Europe ever boasted.'

'Ay, but that little word "if" spoils many a good story,

Ernest. However, though we can at present find no market for these precious things, there is no use in leaving them at the bottom of the sea. Some occasion for bartering them for articles better suited to our circumstances may turn up. In all probability these pearls are unusually perfect. When the bed is rugged and broken, the gems are cloudy and dim; but when smooth and sandy as it is here, they are brilliant and pure.'

'How does it come that it is only in some shells that the jewels are found?' asked Ernest. 'I have read that they are the growth of a certain disease common to the oyster in some latitudes. Can that be the case?'

'It is stated by naturalists,' I replied, 'that pearls are found in oysters, the shells of which have been pierced by a little animal that feeds upon them. In order to stop up the hole made by the hostile parasite, the oyster fills it with a calcar-eous substance which is secreted in its body, and from which the pearl is formed.'

'Are they generally found as near the surface as these are?' questioned Jack. 'If so, they are not hard to obtain, and I wonder at their being so valuable.'

'On the contrary, the work of the pearl-fisher is laborious and dangerous,' I said. 'Sometimes the shells are sixty feet below the surface, and firmly attached to rocks, from which they must be separated with some sharp instrument. They are then thrown into a network basket fastened to the rope which the diver takes down with him, and by means of which he is raised again. The best divers can remain from sixty to eighty seconds in the water, and the chief enemy which they have to dread is the shark. This horrible monster is a common inhabitant of all seas, and many poor men, struggling to obtain a livelihood, fall a prey to it.'

'How much would a fine pearl be worth?' asked Jack.

'The most valuable I have ever seen mentioned was one which Cleopatra, Queen of Egypt, dissolved in a goblet of vinegar and drank at a banquet in honour of Antony. It is stated to have been valued at £52,000.'

'What a terrible fool she must have been,' remarked the impetuous boy warmly. 'If I had been Antony I should not have thanked her much for showing her friendship in that way. But shall we try and obtain a few of these oysters before going away?'

'Most certainly,' I answered; 'though, if we wish to land and explore this part of our territory, we shall not have time to collect many. We must return and gather the chief part of the treasure some other time.'

We spent about an hour in filling a small bag with the largest oysters we could find. Then we sailed cautiously round the foot of the cliffs in search of some spot where we could disembark without trouble. Looking up towards the mighty rocks that towered above us, I was struck by seeing their surface covered with myriads of little nests, about the size of half an egg, and of a light grey colour. Over them fluttered a cloud of brownish-tinted birds, not larger than wrens, that twittered and chirped as if each was trying to drown the noise made by the other.

'Another source of wealth,' I exclaimed. 'This is really a day of priceless discoveries.'

'Why, what sort of birds are those?' asked Ernest. 'They are ugly, insignificant-looking things. It can't be their plumage that makes them valuable.'

'It is not the birds that I refer to,' I said, 'but their nests, with which you see the face of the rock is absolutely hidden.'

'Can it be possible that these are the nests of which so much has been told and written, and for which it is said the Chinese would give almost any money?' questioned the boy further.

'They are indeed,' I replied, 'although I am sure you find it hard to believe, when you look at their rough, unattractive exterior. It is not, however, the nest itself – which is composed of feathers and the filaments of plants – that they esteem as a delicacy, but a little saucer in which it lies, and which is formed of some gelatinous substance. If we had any means of communicating with the inhabitants of the Celestial Empire, we could exchange these saucers for almost anything that we wished, so great is the value placed on them.'

'Let us take home a few to mother,' proposed Jack; 'though they may not tempt her appetite, she will be pleased to see them, and so I am sure will Fritz and Franz.'

In order to procure some of the curiosities, it was necessary to land, and this we were enabled to do only with the help of the cajack, which we had, fortunately, brought with us. To one end of it we fastened a long, thick rope, by which, when it had landed its passenger, we could draw it back to the pinnace that was anchored in the bay. Thus, one by one, we reached the rocky strand, and, mounting the cliffs, carefully detached a few of the nests.

It was so late in the afternoon that we were obliged to abandon all thought of venturing farther inland, for we had promised my wife to be home early, and we knew that if we broke through our arrangement her anxiety would be extreme. Accordingly, we again got on board the pinnace, and turned the prow towards Deliverance Bay.

'I fear there will be a storm before morning,' I said, as I noticed, for the first time, a dark bank of inky clouds lying against the horizon. 'It is fortunate we agreed to return early, else we should not, in all probability, have been able to get back today.'

'I hope we are not about to have a second dose of the squall that overtook us the other day,' remarked Ernest, anxiously. 'The indications of a change in the weather seem much the same as those we observed that afternoon.'

'It strikes me that the wind is rising already,' interposed Jack, looking very wise.

There was little cause for doubt on the subject. The wind sighed mournfully, and the sea heaved restlessly, as if disturbed in its lowest depths.

'In with the sails,' I called, 'and steer straight for the bay. If we strain every muscle, we may win the race yet.'

Higher and higher rose the waves. More threatening grew the clouds, and faster scudded our little vessel before the wind. By degrees darkness enveloped land and sea, and the elements wrestled wildly with each other. Then, suddenly, the whole sky was illuminated, and sheet after sheet of lightning flashed past us with almost blinding brilliancy. Then an instantaneous change took place. The darkness vanished, the wild rocking of the sea subsided, and the evening sun shone brightly in the western heavens. This little squall detained us for more than two hours, and in consequence my wife's alarm had become very great.

Next day we cleaned and polished the pearls that we had gathered, and placed them amongst our valuables, in the expectation that some chance of turning them to account might sooner or later be presented. My wife attempted to utilize the sea-swallows' nests, and placed a bowl of soup before us at dinner; but, with one accord, we pronounced it little short of disgusting, and no further effort was made to enjoy the Chinese delicacy.

CHAPTER XVIII

'A SHIP! A SHIP!'

O F LATE our island had undergone many improvements. Huts had been erected at every spot where we were likely to halt on our expeditions, and cuttings from the European fruit trees planted round them. Our cattle had multiplied almost beyond belief, and numerous sheds had been built for their nightly accommodation. But 'all work and no play' was not our motto, and while expending so much time and labour in bringing about these results, we did not fail to devote an occasional day – or even week – to pleasure-seeking. The Savannah was frequently explored, and the various beautiful and known parts of the island revisited.

On one of our excursions, poor Franz had an encounter which, in all probability, would have had a serious ending but for our faithful friends Topsy and Bill. We were making our way through one of the forests that abounded on the island – the boys, as usual, wandering hither and thither – when I heard the report of a gun, and saw the dogs scampering off. An instant after I was startled by a cry of terror, and, on looking round, saw Franz running at full speed, followed by an animal that was gaining on him at every step. In the excitement of the race, he rushed on, heedless of all obstacles, until he stumbled over the stump of an old tree and fell. His fate seemed sealed, for the wild boar – which the beast turned out to be – was right behind him, and I was unarmed, having left my gun on the cart that Ernest was leading far in front; but our noble dogs perceived their master's danger, and, attacking the animal, drew its anger on themselves. While they were wrestling together, Franz escaped, and a ball from Fritz's gun laid their infuriated antagonist low. When Franz had recovered from his alarm, I thought it right to reprove him for his foolhardiness in attempting to take such a savage brute single-handed.

'I know that, Father,' he said; 'but I had no idea of what the boar was when I went near it. I saw it grubbing in the earth, and regaling itself with what looked like potatoes; so, fancying it was the lost sow, and wishing to see what new dainty she had discovered, I advanced to the place. When the animal saw me, it darted forward; I then fired, but missed; so I took to my heels, thinking that was the surest way of escape.'

'And was it potatoes on which the boar was feeding?'

'I don't know, for I had not time to look, but the spot is quite close to this, and if you come with me, we can soon find out.'

On arriving at the lair of the boar, we found the remains of the vegetables that had formed its last repast.

'What are they?' asked Franz, after regarding them attentively. 'They are not potatoes anyway, I'm sure of that.'

'Oh, no,' I replied; 'they are truffles, and of the most savoury kind.'

'Truffles, truffles,' repeated Jack, as if trying to recall the word to his memory. 'I don't think I ever heard of them before.'

'I don't suppose you did, but nevertheless they are well known and greatly esteemed by Europeans as a choice article of food,' I answered.

'I think the boar must have found the leaves to be the most toothsome part of the vegetable, for there is not a vestige of one left,' interposed Franz.

'I don't doubt that in the least, seeing that they never existed,' was my reply. 'Truffles have no stalk or leaf of any kind, and their presence in the soil is only discovered by the smell. In countries where they are found abundantly, dogs of a certain species are used to search for them. They are attracted by the odour, and sniff and scratch at the place till someone comes with a spade and removes the hidden roots. I have also heard of pigs being kept for the purpose, but as they have a strong partiality for the vegetable, they not unfrequently do a great deal of damage, and help themselves generously to the delicacy.'

We filled a bag with the prized vegetables, and continued on our way. In the evening, seeing it was impossible to reach home with the aid of daylight, we erected the tent on a spot where we had not before encamped. It was just on the bank of a little stream, and, owing to its distance from the forest, we felt sure of passing the night unmolested. When we had lighted a fire, according to our usual custom, and loaded our firearms, we entered the tent, and were about to stretch ourselves on our extemporized bed, when we were startled by a loud roar, which announced the approach of some fear-inspiring foe. The dogs took up the refrain, and howled and whined as if overcome by terror, and even the buffalo added his bass growl to the concert.

'What an awful noise,' muttered Ernest, who, worn out by the fatigue he had endured during the day, was already half asleep, and did not relish the prospect of being disturbed so soon. 'Is the fire burning brightly? If so, we have nothing to fear,' and he rolled over contentedly, and settled himself to sleep.

'The fire is still blazing, but I fear its protection will be very insufficient. If I am not mistaken, our enemy is one which we shall not easily get rid of, and we must take active steps to preserve ourselves,' I replied.

'Why, Father, what do you imagine it is?' asked the boys, now thoroughly roused.

'I believe it is a lion,' was my answer, 'and I also believe that he is not far off.'

I went outside the tent while the boys got their guns ready. On the other side of the stream crouched a lion, whose gigantic form was clearly revealed by the light of the fire that blazed and crackled opposite him. For a while he lay motion-less, gazing fixedly towards us, then rose, and shaking his

mane, as if in aggravation, paced the strand with low majestic tread, never removing his eyes from us. Again he came to a dead stand, and the flame lighted up his fierce, determined face as he stood lashing his sides with his tail in an access of impotent rage. While I was wondering how I ought to act with regard to our unwelcome visitor, a shot rang out behind me, and the huge brute fell, uttering a howl of agony.

'Well done,' I cried, relieved on seeing ourselves freed from the dangerous animal, and delighted to find that Fritz's presence of mind had not forsaken him in the hour of extremity. 'You have accomplished a feat of which any hunter might be proud. The lion's death was so instantaneous that I think you must have hit him through the heart. If you remain here, I will cross the stream, and examine the carcass.'

When I reached the opposite side, which, owing to the shallowness of the water, I was able to do without difficulty,

I found, to my surprise, that Topsy and Bill had preceded me. Ere long I had cause to feel thankful for their companionship; for, just as I was bending over the dead animal, a fine lioness emerged from the darkness, and advanced into the firelight. She roamed restlessly about as if in search of something. Suddenly a mighty roar broke from the enraged beast; she had found her mate. Uttering plaintive cries, she stretched herself beside her dead companion, stroked him with her paws, and licked his wound, wildly glaring round at the same time in search of an object on which to expend her wrath.

The boys had now all gathered in front of the tent, so my dangerous position was not unobserved. Another shot was fired, and the ball lodged in one of the beast's forepaws. The pain only added to her rage. She flung herself with fury on the dogs, and one of the most sanguinary combats I ever witnessed commenced. As I was unarmed, I was incapable of rendering any assistance, and was obliged to remain an inactive spectator of the heart-rending scene. I called to Ernest and Fritz to cross the stream, but before they had done so, a blow from the unwounded paw of the lioness stretched poor Bill on the ground, where he lay in the convulsive agonies of death. The next instant another shot was fired, and the terrible beast rolled over on the sand, never to rise again.

As soon as day had dawned we dug a grave for Bill, and then deprived the two lions of their superb hides, which I promised to stuff as soon as possible. Then we returned to the fortress.

Weeks and months rolled on. Event followed event, adventure succeeded adventure. The summer passed, we spent yet another winter in the grotto, and celebrated our fifth anniversary on the island. My sons had grown into hardy, vigorous young men, with minds well stored with useful knowledge and bodies capable of supporting any amount of fatigue. All of us were enjoying excellent health. Seldom did the thought of deliverance trouble us now. We had grown so accustomed to being separated from our fellow-men, and so used to our present mode of life, that the idea of change rarely occurred to us.

'Were it not for my sons,' my wife would sometimes say, 'I should have no desire to return to Europe. The happiest days of my life have been spent here, and I should like, when dead, to lie under the shade of one of the old trees that sheltered me so often when living. But the thought of leaving my family behind me to die off one by one, untended and uncared for, fills me with dread.'

'The thought is indeed full of bitterness,' I would reply, 'but be of good courage. We shall yet find some means of reaching the land of our birth.' And we looked forward to the future, strong in hope and faith.

The savages, who, as we lately discovered, dwelt on a little peninsula at the farthest extremity of the island, and not on some distant mainland, as we at first thought, had remained invisible for months, and we began to look on our meetings with them almost as a freak of fancy. One evening, however, just as we were on the point of setting out for a short walk, Jack, who had been away alone almost the whole of the day, returned, and told me that he had seen a couple of the natives sneaking about in the vicinity of the fortress. 'They appeared to think we were living there, and waited for some of us to appear,' he said.

'Pooh! Jack, this is another of your cock-and-bull stories,' I remarked incredulously. 'After showing themselves utterly unmindful of our existence for such a length of time, and neglecting so many good opportunities of proving their hostility, they are not going to renew their visits now, I'm sure.'

'I hope not,' he answered; 'but if it was not a pair of savages that I saw hiding in the shrubbery, I'll never trust my eyes again.'

'Put the thought out of your head as fast as you can, and come with us for a stroll,' I suggested.

The shadows of evening were falling over the landscape, and all nature seemed lulled to rest. Only now and again was the silence broken by the good-night song of some feathered chorister, or the bright chirrup of a field cricket in search of its mate. For an hour we rambled about in keen enjoyment of the lovely scene, then turned our steps in the direction of Falcon's Nest, Jack sauntering some distance behind us twisting rods into a whipstick.

When we were within a couple of yards of the tree, a cry of 'The savages! The savages!' roused me from the pleasant reverie into which I had fallen. The shout of alarm had been raised by Ernest, who had gone on before us, and who now stood leaning over the railing which surrounded our dwelling.

'Mount quickly,' he called. 'The red-skins are just beside us. Fast, fast, and let us get ready our arms.'

As he spoke, an arrow whizzed past me, showing that the alarm was no false one, and that the battle had commenced. For about half an hour it raged furiously. The whoops of the savages sounded diabolically in the darkness, and their arrows fell like rain; but as it was impossible for us to distinguish each other, both they and our guns were very ineffective weapons. At last a fearful yell, as of triumph, seemed to go up from the whole band; the arrows ceased to fall, and the crackling of the bushes through which our foes receded proved that for the present the fray was at an end.

'God be praised,' ejaculated my wife, as she sank on a seat, exhausted by the exciting scene she had just passed through. Then – 'But where is Jack?' she asked quickly. No answer came.

'Jack, Jack!' I shouted at the pitch of my voice, thinking he might be hiding somewhere for a joke. 'Jack, answer me, for God's sake'; but still no sound broke the silence.

Fancying one of the arrows might have wounded him, and that he was faint from loss of blood, we searched in every corner of the hut, but no trace of him could be discovered. I then descended to the foot of the tree, in the hope that, seeing himself in a perilous position, he had concealed himself somewhere out of reach of the natives; but my search was fruitless, and my call disregarded.

In perfect agony over the loss of my boy, I set out with his brothers to look for him. All night we wandered up and down, but morning dawned without our having found any clue to his disappearance, and we returned to the Nest faint from grief and exhaustion.

'The natives must have got hold of him,' I said. 'Get ready the pinnace, Ernest. Put all our guns and a couple of extra cannon on board. I mean to start immediately.'

Despite all my wife's entreaties to be allowed to accompany me, I decided to leave her and Franz at home, knowing what danger they would incur should we meet face to face with our enemies.

Three hours elapsed before we rounded the point on which the huts of the savages stood – hours that passed like years. As we sailed along slowly, looking for a safe harbour in which to anchor, Fritz called excitedly, 'Look, there they are, just on the top of the cliff. Let us push out a little, and fire before they see us.'

Sure enough, right above us stood a group of about twenty savages, engaged in, as far as I could judge, by their energetic gestures, a most earnest and warm discussion.

'If we fire now, we should in all probability only wound one or two, and the others would station themselves so as to prevent our landing without serious opposition,' I said. 'I think it is wiser to gain the strand if possible, before they become aware of our presence.'

As I spoke, a wild cry rang through the air, followed by a loud splash.

'They have seen us,' I cried to the boys. 'They have seen us. Fire!'

Time after time our cannon boomed, and the reports, mingled with the terrified cries of the natives, were echoed from rock and cave.

Suddenly, amid the confusion of sounds, I seemed to hear someone calling faintly, 'Father, father, save me,' and I perceived a dark head appearing above the water at some distance from us.

'Can that be Jack?' I asked, as I looked in doubt at the swimmer, who was nearing us slowly, and with apparent difficulty.

'It is, it is!' shouted Ernest. 'Saved, saved!' and as the cry of 'Father' again rang out, all doubt was removed.

In a few minutes we had him on board, but the danger that he had just escaped had been so great that he fainted in my arms. While we were occupied in trying to restore him to consciousness, I observed a small canoe, occupied by two men, pushing out from the shore and steering in our direction. As soon as it came near, its occupants waved a white flag as a sign that their visit was made with friendly intentions, and, though my faith in their friendship and honour was of the weakest, I allowed them to come close to us without making any hostile preparations for their reception. What was my surprise to see that one of the boatmen had the fair skin of a European, though his scant clothing and the blotches of paint with which his body was ornamented showed that civilization had been forgotten, and that he had joined himself to the ranks of his savage brethren. When we were within speaking distance, he hailed me in Italian. Fortunately my knowledge of that language enabled me to understand and answer him.

'We are friends,' he called. 'Will you receive us as such? We did our best to save your boy. Trust us, and you will not find yourself deceived.'

'I will trust you,' I answered; 'but if you betray that trust, your life will be the penalty.'

'Agreed,' he said. 'Will you allow us on board your vessel until we explain what has lately occurred?'

I gave the required permission, and in a few minutes he and his companion, whom as yet no word had escaped, stepped on deck. The smile of understanding and recognition that passed between them and Jack, who was almost restored, served to remove all my suspicions, and I listened attentively to the story that the Italian began to relate.

'My name,' he said, 'is Auferi. I was captain of a vessel that was driven out of its course by a storm, and wrecked twelve years ago on this island. Not another soul escaped with his life. I was thrown on the shore in an unconscious state, and was found there by a few natives, whose good opinion was bought by my watch and some other pieces of jewellery that I had about my person. As well as presenting them with these, which seemed to them priceless treasures, I gained their respect by proving to them that I was not devoid of courage and daring, and I brought them to look on me as a magician, or something similar, by the performance of a few juggler's tricks that I had learned when a boy. In this way I obtained a certain influence amongst them, even at first; by degrees I rose, until I am now one of the chiefs of the tribe. My good friend, Taliti, whom you see here beside me, is next to me in power, and our united influence is greater than that of Owaihu, our king. Your presence on the island has been the source of much dissension in our camp. Owaihu and his followers were determined to destroy you and seize your possessions, but Taliti and I managed to thwart them. Sometimes they acted with excessive cunning and secrecy, and got off without our knowledge. One of these occasions was last night, when your son came near falling a victim to their hatred.'

'But did they really mean to kill him?' I asked breathlessly. 'Surely they could not have been so cruel?'

'It was almost by chance that an hour ago he was not pierced by a dozen arrows,' was the reply. 'This is the day of our national feast, and it is our custom to celebrate it by the shedding of blood. I asked Owaihu this morning what victim he had prepared, but his answers were as unsatisfactory as those of an oracle; and it was only when Jack was led forth from the hut in which he had been concealed that I guessed of the attack that had been so successfully made last night. The sight of the white face of the boy, and the supplicating looks which he cast on me, seeing that I differed in appearance from my companions, touched my heart, and made me determine to save him, should my own life pay for his. Good Taliti joined in my determination. We implored Owaihu to relinquish his cruel design, and restore the innocent boy to his home; but our entreaties were received with bursts of anger, and he swore that the white boy's blood should colour the soil.

'"It may, but it will be mingled with that of others," I muttered in desperation, and I signed to those who were on our side to station themselves close to me. To my surprise, a large majority of our companions expressed their intention of going against the king, and Owaihu stood looking on his meagre band of followers, rage and dismay pictured on his countenance. The fight was just about to commence when Jack, from whose hands and feet I had a few minutes before removed the ropes with which they were bound, saw your little vessel, and with a sudden resolve to trust himself to the sea when you were near, darted to the edge of the cliff and threw himself into the water. The cannon which you then turned on us did deadly work. Several of our band are lying on the hill bathed in blood; amongst them is Owaihu. He will trouble you no more. And now, as chief of the tribe, Taliti and I proffer you our friendship. Will you accept it?'

The recital had so moved me that for a short time I remained speechless. Then rising, I embraced the two men warmly. To them I owed the life of my son, and my heart went out in love and gratitude towards them.

'Henceforth,' said I, 'let us live at peace with one another. I acknowledge you to be my friends and benefactors, and time will never wipe out the remembrance of the debt I owe you.'

With mutual expressions of esteem we parted. Auferi and Taliti returned to their camp, and we sailed back to Deliverance Bay, eager to make known to my wife the good news of Jack's rescue.

The next day ambassadors arrived from our newly-made friends, and presented to us, in the name of the tribe, and in token of their peace and goodwill, offerings of furs, coral, feathers, and shells. I received the messengers warmly, entertained them hospitably, and sent them back to their chiefs laden with knives, guns, jewellery, and other articles of European manufacture which I knew they would look on as priceless treasure.

From this time our intercourse was of the friendliest description, and many pleasant evenings were spent by us in the company of Auferi, who frequently came and passed a day or two with us, and of whom the boys became exceedingly fond. We, in our turn, often visited the encampment of the natives, and gained the affections of the whole band by the presents of beads and other worthless trifles which we always took with us and distributed amongst them.

One evening, as we were about to leave Shark Island, where we had spent the day in making some improvements about the watch-tower, Ernest, who was scanning the horizon with his telescope, shouted, 'A ship, a ship! I can't be mistaken. Look towards the north.'

The excitement caused by this announcement was intense, and my hands trembled so violently that I could hardly hold the glass; but by resting it on Fritz's shoulder, I was able to distinguish a vessel speeding along with all sails spread.

'Hoist the signals,' I cried. 'Fire the cannon. Do everything in the power of man to attract attention.'

'But they may be pirates,' suggested my wife, struggling between hope and fear, 'and their approach may cause us sorrow rather than joy. Better let them pass.'

'Remember your anxiety about our sons' future,' I said. 'Remember their loneliness when we are gone. It is possible our signals may not be seen, or that the ship may look upon a nearer approach as dangerous; but let us, nevertheless, do our best to make them observe us.'

With straining eyes and wildly beating hearts we gazed towards the vessel round which all our hopes centred, and which promised to deliver or doom us to lifelong exile. At last it seemed as if the prow were turned in our direction; but this we could not feel assured of till the boom of one of the ship's cannon proved beyond a doubt that our signals had not escaped their notice. On they came, nearer and nearer, and hope and fear contended in our bosoms.

Suddenly Fritz cried, 'We are saved! We are saved! The red, white, and blue flag of England is floating at the mast-head.'

The vessel, which turned out to be the *Maritana*, commanded by Captain Parker, cast anchor in the bay, and from it a boat was lowered, into which several men stepped, and rowed towards us. I entered the pinnace, accompanied by Ernest and Fritz, and advanced to meet them. As we drew near, a hearty cheer went up from the boat's occupants; their fears of treachery were banished, for our complexions contradicted the impression given by our curious garb, and they saw that we were Europeans. As soon as we came alongside each other, the captain stood up and asked who we were, and how we had come to be on the island. His limited knowledge of French, and my slight acquaintance with English, conversationally, rendered an explanation somewhat difficult, but I contrived to make him understand the story of the shipwreck and our miraculous escape. My short and imperfect sketch of our adventures interested him deeply, and he expressed a desire to hear a detailed account of them. In order to have his wish gratified, he rowed back to the ship and brought from it one of the passengers – Mr. Wolstone by name – who was thoroughly conversant with my native language, and through whom the captain and I were enabled to satisfy our curiosity respecting each other.

I joyfully welcomed the strangers to my kingdom, and

begged them to remain for a few days as my guests until they should have procured those things which they had need of, and my family and I had made our necessary preparations for quitting the land where we had dwelt so long. For now that the means of returning to a civilized country were placed within our reach, we did not for a moment doubt the expediency of seizing them. Though my wife and I would willingly have spent the remainder of our days on that island, where we had suffered and learned so much, we could not think for a moment of condemning our family longer to an exile of which they, particularly Ernest and Jack, had grown wearied.

The captain and Mr. Wolstone readily accepted my invitation, and soon were lodged in the Fortress – that dwelling which the lavish hand of Nature had provided for us. For a couple of days my time was fully occupied in displaying the beauties of my dominion to my admiring companions; and while we made our short excursions, my wife and the boys collected our various portable possessions with all haste, and packed them up, ready for transmission to the ship, which lay at anchor within the shelter of the bay.

On the evening of the second day after the arrival of our deliverers, I observed that Mr. Wolstone was unusually silent, and seemed to be revolving some serious project in his mind. The captain rallied him often on what he called his 'fit of melancholy', but his railleries failed to provoke an explanation. At last he roused himself from his reverie, and, turning to me, quickly asked, 'Are you quite resolved to return to Europe? I should fancy you must think of quitting this spot with intense regret.'

'I do that,' I replied. 'Nothing but an earnest desire to promote the happiness and prosperity of our children could induce either myself or my wife to abandon New Switzerland. But, as I told you before, Ernest and Jack are most anxious to change their mode of life, now that the opportunity is available. Fritz and Franz are never so happy as when engaged in those pursuits from which they will be entirely cut off when dwelling in a civilized land; so their regret at leaving will be almost as great as my own. If I saw any probability of our island ever coming under the notice of and proving attractive to emigrants, I should not think of quitting it.'

When I had finished, Mr. Wolstone remained for a moment lost in thought. Then, raising his head, he said: 'If lack of companionship is your only reason for resolving to return to the old country, you may abandon the determination at once, at least for the present; for I have made up my mind to take up my abode on this island for a while, and if I find the climate to be as healthful and pleasant as I imagine I shall, I mean to spend the remainder of my days here with my wife and daughters, who are on board the *Maritana*.'

'Do you really mean it?' cried my wife, as, trembling with excitement, she rose from her chair, and stood beside Mr. Wolstone.

'I do, indeed,' he replied. 'As your husband has doubtless told you, I was ordered by my physicians to leave England and try to regain my lost health in that land for which our vessel is bound. This I was told was my only chance of life. The sea voyage, however, has restored me almost completely, and your home here pleases me so much that I have decided to go no farther, provided you also remain. My wife, with whom I talked the matter over last night, is as anxious as I am to disembark on this favoured spot, and my daughters are sighing for the moment when they may leave the vessel and pay a visit to the island of which I have told them so much.'

The boys no sooner heard this than they bounded off with a loud 'hurrah', and the next thing I saw was them unmooring the pinnace and sailing gaily towards the *Maritana*. In the course of an hour they returned, bringing with them Mrs. Wolstone and her two daughters, Alice and Mary, aged respectively sixteen and twelve. My wife and I received them warmly, and gave expression to our unfeigned joy over their resolve. The evening was spent in relating past experiences, and picturing bright visions of our future happiness.

When our visitors had returned to the vessel for the night, I called Ernest and Jack to me, and questioned them earnestly regarding their desires. With reluctance I got them to acknowledge that their wish to visit Europe was still very strong, and I determined to place no obstacle in their way. The various expenses which they must necessarily incur could be defrayed by a portion of the money which I had found on the wreck, and which Captain Parker declared to be legally mine. That night, therefore, my wife set about getting their scanty wardrobe in order, for it was decided that on the following evening the ship should once more proceed on her interrupted course.

Next morning the possessions of Mr. Wolstone and his family were transferred to our abode, and the light boxes belonging to Ernest and Jack sent back in the boat.

As the afternoon crept on our spirits sank, and the thought of parting with our sons for a time oppressed us heavily. Auferi and Taliti, to whom we had conveyed the news of the change in our arrangements, arrived at the Fortress, and showed by their troubled looks that they participated in our grief. At length the ship's bell rang, the last good-byes were said, and the boys, with Captain Parker, stepped into the boat that awaited them, and rowed towards the vessel. In a few minutes a loud cheer burst from the ship's crew, as the anchor was weighed, and the *Maritana* set sail. Ere darkness had completely closed in around us, the quickly-receding vessel had disappeared below the horizon, and miles of sea rolled between us and our two boys.

Four years afterwards Ernest returned from Europe, accompanied by a fair young wife, and settled down once more in the old home. Jack, for whom the adventurous career of a sailor had irresistible attractions, could not be persuaded to abandon his roving life. 'I am not made for a family man,' he would say, with a touch of his old roguery, as he looked at Fritz, who, he saw every reason to suspect, was about to follow Ernest's example, and introduce another member into the family. Nor were his suspicions unfounded. A few months later, Alice Wolstone and Fritz were married, and comfortably ensconced in a new dwelling that I had built for them at Prospect Hill.

Mr. Wolstone's health was now completely restored, but the home of his adoption had become so dear to him that the thought of leaving it was never entertained for a moment; and when Jack sometimes proposed that he should accompany him back to Europe, he would say, 'No, no, you can present my compliments to the old country, but the spot that now is and ever will be dearest to my heart is the beautiful island of New Switzerland.'

JOHANN DAVID WYSS (1743–1818) was, like the narrator of his famous story of survival on an uninhabited island, a Swiss pastor who had four sons. It was to entertain and instruct these children that he devised the idea of the island and its plethora of natural resources, but the writing of *Der schweizerische Robinson* is said to have been the responsibility of one of the sons, Johann Rudolf (1782–1830). First published in 1812, it was first translated into English two years later. Since then its translators have been many and they have freely adapted and expanded the original German text, making it one of the most popular novels of all time.

LOUIS JOHN RHEAD (1857–1926), an American artist, was born in England. He illustrated many classics of children's literature, including *Gulliver's Travels* (1913), Grimms' Fairy Tales (1917) and Stevenson's *Kidnapped* (1921), all for the firm of Harper in New York. His illustrations for *The Swiss Family Robinson*, 'done from sketches made in the tropics', were first published in 1909.

ROALD DAHL *The BFG*
Illustrated by Quentin Blake

DANIEL DEFOE *Robinson Crusoe*
Illustrated by W. J. Linton and others

CHARLES DICKENS *A Christmas Carol*
Illustrated by Arthur Rackham

SIR ARTHUR CONAN DOYLE *Sherlock Holmes*
Illustrated by Sidney Paget

RICHARD DOYLE *Jack the Giant Killer*
Illustrated by Richard Doyle

ALEXANDRE DUMAS *The Three Musketeers*
Illustrated by Edouard Zier

C. S. EVANS *Cinderella*
The Sleeping Beauty
Illustrated by Arthur Rackham

JEAN DE LA FONTAINE *Fables*
Illustrated by R. de la Nézière

OLIVER GOLDSMITH, WILLIAM COWPER and OTHERS
Ride a-Cock-Horse and other
Rhymes and Stories
Illustrated by Randolph Caldecott

KENNETH GRAHAME *The Wind in the Willows*
Illustrated by Arthur Rackham

THE BROTHERS GRIMM *Fairy Tales*
Illustrated by Arthur Rackham

NATHANIEL HAWTHORNE *A Wonder-Book*
Illustrated by Arthur Rackham

FRANCES HODGSON BURNETT *The Secret Garden*
Illustrated by Charles Robinson

Little Lord Fauntleroy
Illustrated by C. E. Brock

ROBERT LOUIS STEVENSON *A Child's Garden of Verses*
Illustrated by Charles Robinson

Kidnapped
Illustrated by Rowland Hilder

Treasure Island
Illustrated by Mervyn Peake

JEAN WEBSTER *Daddy-Long-Legs*
Illustrated by the Author

OSCAR WILDE *The Happy Prince and
other Tales*
Illustrated by Charles Robinson

JOHANN WYSS *The Swiss Family Robinson*
Illustrated by Louis Rhead